R.R.R.
ROGUE RIVER ROY

BY
DR. LEWIS R. CANNON, B.S.

ISBN: 978-0-9793514-1-9
First Printing March 2007

WEGFERDS' PRINTING & PUBLICATIONS
Cover by Karen Wegfahrt
North Bend, OR 97459

Printed in the U.S.A.

INTRODUCTION

This book is a collection of stories about Rogue River Roy and his many friends. Some are taken from his journal, others are stories he told around the campfire. All the facts are as accurate and truthful as Folk Tale Fiction permits.

The descriptions of some characters have been repeated as each individual tale must stand on its own.

Some names have been changed to protect the guilty. Some names have not been changed to punish the guilty. No one is innocent.

This book was written for my grandchildren and perhaps to bring a smile to a face I've never seen.

Lewis Cannon
A.K.A. Ari Resseh
Shadow Man

ACKNOWLEDGEMENT

I would like to thank Jessica Bryan
for her hard work in editing this piece.
Her help was invaluable.
Also Patricia Melvin, she helped me git 'ur
done. Determined to see it finished.

TABLE OF CONTENTS

DEDICATION

Patricia Melvin has been encouraging
me for years to write my stories and
has helped this semi-literate bone head tirelessly.
I am deeply indebted to her for her tireless
devotion in publishing my books.

With love and gratitude
I. F. Hessler

PROLOGUE

What I am about to tell you cannot be repeated, or the secret will be out and the great gold rush will begin. Remember, this is a story about a man's life, not the greatest gold discovery ever made. Focus on the man, not the gold.

It all started a few years back when I was fishing the Rogue River, just above "Secret Bar." A big steelhead took my homemade fly and started upstream. He broke my three-pound leader without even looking back. How contemptuous; I hate an arrogant fish. Now I can't tell you the pattern I was using, but it pretty well matched the hatch in progress with a little "extra."

I knew that ornery lunker was up in the next pool laughing at me, but he was out of range of any cast I could muster. The bank was a shear rock wall about eight hundred feet high, but I had to have another go at that smug monster.

A steep rockslide ended in the middle of Secret Bar and it just might offer a way around. I started up the slide, slipping, falling and starting a small landslide with every step, but I was determined to get around the cliff so I could get down to that next gravel bar.

After struggling for about an hour, I came to a little ledge that led off upstream. It was not very wide mind you, just enough to allow passage. I had to face the cliff with my left foot pointing downstream and my right foot pointing upstream. Like a crab, I began to inch along this narrow path, if one could call this goat trail a "path."

The weight of the pack on my back caused me to lean forward so there wasn't any clearance for the brim of my hat. There I was, hat in my left hand, fishing pole in my right, inching along. What a guy won't do for a chance at a big fish.

I guess I had crabbed along in this fashion for about two hundred feet, when I came to a little alder tree growing out of a crack in the solid rock. I figured I could just press against it till it broke and I could get by. Boy was I wrong! The more I pressed, the more it pressed back. Now with both hands full I started to fall backwards. At the point when I knew I was going to fall and couldn't do anything about it, I decided I would rather land on my feet than my head. I did a back flip, just like I used to do at the old swimming hole. I thought I was in for a hard landing, but I came down on a little flat spot about ten feet below and crashed right through the ground into a dark cave.

I stood in the dust and debris unable to see, afraid to move. Soon my eyes became accustomed to the dark. With the light from the hole I had just created, I could see I was in a room of sorts. I fumbled for my Everdry match safe I always kept my wood matches in and struck one on the seat of my jeans, as I usually do. When the match flared, the first thing I noticed was the Sunday Comics. They were pasted all over the walls of a room about twelve feet square and six feet high.

I know for a fact that the early pioneers used to mix flour and water to make a paste and then use it to put newspaper over the cracks in the walls to keep out the wind and cold. The dates on some of the comics pasted on these walls ranged from 1898 to 1902. I recognized the *Toonerville Trolley* and the *Captain and the Kids*, even before they left Germany.

There was a Hudson wood and coal stove with an oven and cook-top against the east wall. A half-filled wood box with a grate shaker handle placed on top, to the left. The south wall had two built-in bunks. A couple of colorful, striped, Hudson Bay wool blankets lay folded at the foot. An oil lantern hung by its bail from a spike driven into the main support beam. The east wall held shelves made from rough cedar planks, floor to ceiling, with boxes, tins and canvas bags crowding each other for space. To the right of the shelves there was a door with a small, dirt-coated window that was covered by a worn piece of canvas. The door was nailed shut and the window boarded over. An old leather holster hung on a peg near the door; the butt of a revolver sticking out of it. My pulse quickened. Could it be an Army Colt revolver? "Yes!" I shouted with joy. It was just like the one that my granddad had many years ago. If there was one thing I wanted in this world, it was an 1851 "Army Colt." How could a guy get so lucky?

As I drew the six-gun from the holster, I was disappointed to see a little rust wherever the gun had

touched the leather. I could almost hear my father saying, "Never leave a firearm in a leather holster or scabbard – whatever they tan the hide with will ruin the metal, and if you do I'll tan your hide." All in all, it was in great condition and would clean up just fine.

A small table and two benches were placed near the center of the room close to the hole I had created by my acrobatic entrance. In the center of the table was the stub of a candle on top of an old wax-dripped bottle. I struck another match and lit the candle, picked up the bottle, and moved to the north wall. A piece of dusty canvas covered the wall. As I pulled up a corner of the crusty cloth, I was surprised to see a mine entrance, or "drift," in the solid rock wall.

A collection of tools, picks, star-drills, rock-hammers and six cases of dynamite set just inside the entrance. Nitroglycerin formed shining beads of sweat on the outside of the boxes, matching the ones forming on my forehead. The dynamite was very unstable and so was I. My mind screamed, "Get out! Get out! Get out!" I lowered the canvas, started to breathe again, and sat down on one of the benches.

While I sat there thinking about leaving the cabin, I noticed a five-pound biscuit tin in an old wooden box nailed to the wall. There was a little rust on it, but the painted picture and writing was still visible. Next to the tin was a Mason jar that contained many wild turkey quills, all most-likely prepared with the little gold penknife that lay close by. The container was covered with a coating that smelled faintly of beeswax. I used my pocketknife to scrape around the lid and gently pried it off.

Inside was something that would change my life forever: a leather-bound book wrapped in oilcloth. I moved to the table and after wiping off the dust and dirt with my shirtsleeve, I sat down to read. I opened the book carefully and turned to the title page, where I saw written in large bold letters:

R. R. R.
THE LIFE AND TIMES OF ROGUE RIVER ROY
Born October 3, 1833 –

The man must have had some education, because there was even a Table of Contents listing each chapter. It looked like some very exciting reading and I was soon totally engrossed. I lost all track of time as I followed the vivid descriptions of fantastic events that made up the life of this mysterious man. Each chapter was a separate adventure and there were over a hundred of them in the large, handwritten book. There didn't seem to be much rhyme or reason to their order. Some were tall tales and some were just stories for fun; still others resembled Aesop's Fables, each with a lesson to be learned. The penmanship was excellent ("Palmer" would have been proud).

I suddenly found it difficult to read and realized the sun must have set. Well, that meant I was stuck here for the rest of the night. There was a tin of candles on one of the shelves, so I lit two, placed them on the table in a puddle of their own wax and continued reading long into the night . . . .

Later, I felt a little draft and the candle flickered. I froze in near terror as the canvas covering the mine entrance began to rise.

First I saw the boots – a style from many years past. A pocket for a small clasp knife was sewn on the outside of the right boot. Thick red wool stockings were rolled down over the boot tops. Next there was a pair of coarse canvas pants, maybe homemade, with patches on both knees. A pair of wide, yellow suspenders held them up on the outside of a red and black-checkered wool shirt. Large, powerful hands poked out of each half-rolled-up sleeve. Next came a craggy face with all the character of a long, hard, no-nonsense life etched there deeply – furrow after furrow of wrinkles added their testimony.

I could see the anger rising in those penetrating, steel blue eyes. His white beard hardly covered the color change from pink to fuming red as he glanced at the hole in the roof. Then, when he saw I was reading his journal, he began to vibrate with increasing intensity. I sat there transfixed by that fearsome expression, waiting for the explosion that was sure to follow.

But, at that moment, a great calmness seemed to come over him. It was as if he had just thought of a solution to all his problems. A twinkle appeared in his blue eyes, which belied the seeming severity of the creature that stood before me. I realized I had stopped breathing when the canvas had first started to move. I gasped for air as the specter spoke!

"BOO!" he said, and boy did I jump!

"Did you ever see a critter caught in a trap when you first walk up on him and he knows he's had it? Well, that's what you look like, sonny. Like a skunk caught in a trap!"

He slapped his knee and started to laugh. *More like a cackle*, I thought.

The ancient one turned and with a motion of his hand beckoned me to follow. I did as he indicated. Past the canvas covering the entrance to the mine there was a lit coal oil lamp, just like the one carried by the old miner. I took it off the nail and hurried to catch up to him. Deep into the mountain we went, following a vein of quartz that must have been twenty inches wide – the biggest I had ever heard of or seen.

After traveling about four hundred feet, we came to a solid wall with a deep pool of water in front of it. If you have ever been in a mine or cave you know the water is crystal clear because there's no wind or critters to stir it up.

The old timer sat down on an empty dynamite

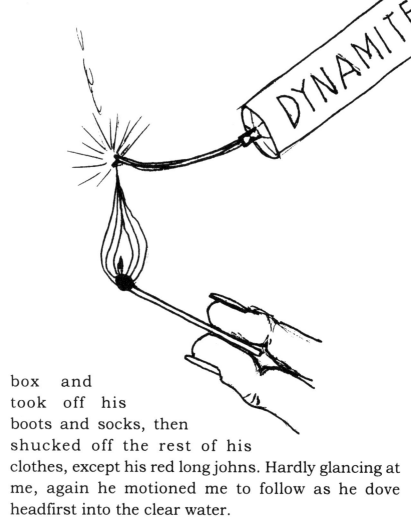

box   and
took   off   his
boots and socks, then
shucked off the rest of his
clothes, except his red long johns. Hardly glancing at
me, again he motioned me to follow as he dove
headfirst into the clear water.

I hung my lantern on a peg beside his, took off
all my clothes and stood there looking into that
shimmering pool. I really did not want to do this, but
I took a few deep breaths and launched myself after
the old miner.

I swam along following the bottom where I saw
box after box filled with gold. So this is where he

stashed all his hard-worked-for treasure, the sly old devil. As I surfaced, I saw him towel off with a flour sack and then start to dress in clothes similar to the ones he had left on the other side of the pool. He turned toward me and again beckoned me to follow. He took one of the lanterns from a peg driven into a crack and lumbered off deeper into the mine.

I slipped on a pair of worn-out boots, wrapped one of the old flour sacks around me and continued following this strange character. I came upon him as he faced away from me, bent over, doing something at the end of the drift. I looked over his shoulder just as he struck a match to a fuse that led to five other fuses, which then led to many more. The acid smoke stung my nostrils as the fuse sputtered and flashed. I stood there frozen, my mind spinning with what was happening.

The old man turned and started that frightening laugh of his. It was time to vamoose and I took off running as fast as I could go. Actually faster than that, more like a jackrabbit being chased by a hungry coyote. I reached the pool and dove in head first without taking off my boots. I did my underwater speed stroke, even managing to swipe a couple of nuggets as I flashed by the boxes of gold. I surfaced grabbing my clothes on the go when the explosion hit. BANG!

BANG! My head hit the table and I woke up in a sweat. My pulse hammered in my head. The faint light of dawn was coming through the roof. The candles were mere puddles. Had it all been a dream?

I had not eaten since yesterday and boy was I starved. Upon opening my pack, I found a little jerky and one of yesterday's biscuits. As I sat there eating my breakfast, I looked up and saw the initials R. R. R. on the main support beam. They looked like they had been branded by a hot poker many years before. "Well, I'll be!" I said aloud. "I bet he used to sit at this very table and write in his journal or play cards or swap yarns. Well, I'll be."

It was time to leave, so I moved the table under the hole in the roof and placed one of the benches on top. As I stood on the bench, I noted the construction of the roof. Heavy cedar planks, now somewhat rotted, were double-lapped and covered by two layers of tarpaper. This was followed by an inch of clay and a few inches of pea gravel. On top of it all were just plain dirt, grass and brush making the cabin all but invisible. So that was why everything in this old shack was dry and well preserved, sealed until now – not bad for forty years.

I shoved my "Trapper Nelson" pack up onto the roof and managed to crawl after it. I noticed some steps cut into the rock face of the cliff. They led down to the back door and I followed them up to the little ledge that had started me on this strange adventure. I managed to get back to Secret Bar after sliding down that rocky slope. It was more like a series of controlled falls.

No sooner did I head down river than it started to rain. I left Secret Bar behind me with no time to dally. I knew the river would start to rise and the fall rains signaled the beginning of a gloomy winter approaching. It had been a great summer. I had fished every day since the first of June and now it was time to do some serious work. My dad had a good friend who had mined this area for years. He was a real expert when it came to explosives. Maybe he would partner up with me and we could explore the old mine together.

The rain didn't slack off a bit. In fact, it just kept coming down harder and harder. By the time I got back to town, the river was up over two feet and rising fast. It was very unusual for an early fall rainstorm.

Well, it didn't let up for over two weeks and my plan to go back upriver just wasn't going to happen. There was a full-blown flood, the worst anyone had seen in forty years. My cabin sat high on the north bank of the Rogue River out of any danger. There was so much junk and debris coming down the river – it was unbelievable.

The next morning, the sky was blue with hardly a cloud anywhere. This would be a good day to walk the beach and look for firewood. The river was still up and probably wouldn't go down for a couple days. Luckily, it was a minus tide. I had never seen so much drift on the beach – ever. I was stumbling through the driftwood when something vaguely familiar caught my eye. It was a large timber roughly hewn. When I rolled it over I saw the marking R. R. R.! The end of the beam looked as if it had been shattered in an explosion. I was shattered, too. My dream of revisiting the gold mine disappeared, just as that little cabin must have vanished in a flash. Probably some animal fell through the hole in the roof and set the whole thing off. Well, no use crying over spilt milk. I just had to get over it. At least I still had the old Army Colt and the journal. Maybe I'll publish it fifty years from now so everyone will know about Rogue River Roy.

I thought it would be a good idea to wait until the lust for gold had disappeared and we could focus on the man, not the gold. So, that's exactly what I've done. It's been fifty years since I fell through that cabin roof and now here are some of the stories from the journal of R. R. R.

Lewis Cannon

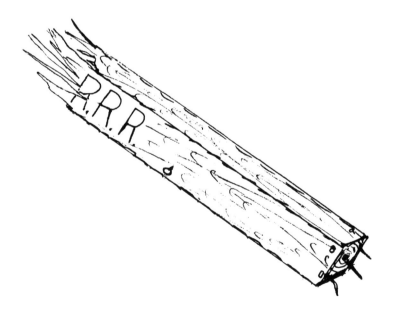

TALE ONE
SNORING
RATTLESNAKES

It was late one fall, about mid-December and I was on my way back to the gold mine. I had picked up some flour, coffee, salt, pepper and other provisions to see me through the winter. I'd left Gold Beach early that morning and was already climbing Wild Cat Ridge. The first thing I saw when I topped the ridge was some very dark clouds coming in fast from the north.

Not just a squall, mind you, but serious, black, boiling, rip-snorting clouds. They were so black that when a crow took off flying against them he looked white!

I thought I had plenty of time to make it to a line shack a couple miles up the trail, but I was in for a big surprise. When cresting the next ridge, I was knocked over backwards, flattened by a cold wind blowing over two hundred miles an hour.

And snow! I'll tell you about snow. When I started to fall backwards, there wasn't a single flake on the ground anywhere. But by the time I landed, there was four feet of snow everywhere, but it cushioned my fall. Not only that, but I made a human snowball rolling down that hill – till I crashed into a rock wall about half way down.

I didn't need a soothsayer to tell me I was in serious trouble unless I could get out of this confounded wind. I took out the old Bowie knife that I use for just about everything and started to dig in. It wasn't long till I discovered a small opening at the base of the wall and succeeded in making it big enough to crawl through.

By this time, the snow was eight feet deep, about a foot a minute. Now, that's not a record for these parts, but darn close.

I took my pack off and shoved it through the hole ahead of me, then crawled about ten feet into the total darkness. Being worn out by all that digging, I just pulled a blanket out of my pack, curled up and went to sleep.

*   *   *

When I awoke, I felt pressure all over me as though I was covered with snow, but I wasn't cold. Then there was this horrible snoring sound, like a hundred little buzz saws. It was so dark I couldn't see my hand in front of my face. (So this is what they mean by "pitch black.")

I felt for the little corked medicine bottle I kept my wood matches in and struck one on my teeth. I still couldn't see a thing so I struck another match and sure enough the first one was lit, only it was just too dark to see the light.

To my great shock, I discovered I was covered with snoring rattlesnakes from head to foot. Very slowly, I eased out from under my blanket and shook it. Then I stepped back deeper into the cave. Most of the snoring stopped for a few seconds, but soon they were all back at it, all sound asleep and snoring.

After rummaging around in my pack, I found the stub of a candle that gave me enough light to see a huge pack-rat nest about eight feet high. It only took a minute to get a small fire going with a few sticks from the nest. I noticed that the smoke drifting towards the back of the cave and thought I'd take a look-see.

With my candle to guide me, I started to explore the cave and found a small drip of water coming off the ceiling. *Well, I'll just put my tin coffee cup under it and catch enough water to keep me goin' till I can get out of here,* I thought. After moving another thirty feet or so, I heard more snoring – deep ponderous snoring – more like a low roar. The hair on the back of my neck rose up as my pulse quickened. My flickering candle revealed a room full of sleeping grizzly bears in deep hibernation. There must've been a dozen of 'em.

With my heart pounding in my throat, I backed quietly, very quietly, out of the bear-filled den. Whew, what a pickle I was in, rattle-snakes on one side and grizzly bears on the other. I went back to the fire to try and figure a way out of the trap I had gotten myself into.

As the fire-warmed things up a bit, the closest snake quit snoring and started shaking his rattle as he moved towards me. He was angry and very excited. I was just very excited.

When that first rattler struck I was ready for him. I hacked off his head in mid-strike with my Bowie knife. I was getting down right hungry by then, so I skinned him rolled him in a little flour, fried him and ate a mighty fine breakfast.

That pretty well set the pattern for the days to come. The solution to my problem was to eat my way out. There were a hundred and thirty-three snakes between me and freedom. With eighty feet of snow outside and plenty of food and water, I was in good shape to weather the storm.

It was the first of March by the time I had eaten my way out of there. Just as the last of the snow was melting, those durn grizzly bears started to wake up. A big old silverback went on a rampage as soon as he got a whiff of me. I heard him roaring as he began his search.

It was going to be close. I blew out my candle so he couldn't see me and I pushed my pack through the hole I had widened. I felt his horrible breath on my neck as I scrambled through the opening. His massive jaws clamped down on my boot as he tried to pull me back into the cave. I felt him dragging me backwards. I put my other foot on the rock wall and pushed with all my might. I was still losing the tug of war. Then I reached back and pulled the throwing knife out of my boot and started to cut the leather laces. With a loud pop I fell backwards, head over heels.

Suddenly I was free! Those powerful jaws had snapped the heel off my boot. The old silverback had his head half out of the hole. His vicious-looking teeth snapping in anger at his lost prey. Lucky for me the entrance was too small for him to follow or I'd been a goner.

Now, I'd have to go back to town and get my boot fixed at Stitch's Bootery. Boy, I'll have something to say about his boots not holdin' up to a playful little grizzly.

The only problem I got out of the whole ordeal was one leg was four inches longer than the other. I walked in circles a lot – till it shrunk back to normal.

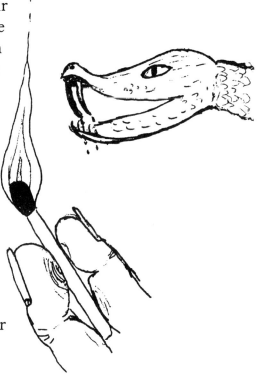

Sometimes I think maybe I should'a ate myself out the other way, but then I wouldn't of had one hundred and thirty-three rattles to sell to the flatland foreigners, only some old bear claws. And yes! Rattlesnake does taste just like chicken. However, my tastes have changed somewhat since then.

TALE TWO
THE BULLY, BOGUS BILLY BOGGS

It felt good to be on the trail again, to leave the stuffiness of town behind and smell the scent of the Myrtle trees blowing on the pre-dawn breeze. There was still a little chill in the air and I could hear the girls behind me breathing heavy as we were about to crest the first ridge after leaving town. A great spring day was beginning and soon the morning sun would warm my face when we arrived at the summit. It's the little pleasures one looks forward to when you live a simple life.

Before we started winding down the other side, I thought I'd give the mules a short rest in the little mountain meadow that the trail cut through. It's always nice to take a break after your first sweat of the day – you kinda get a second wind and then you're good for the rest of the day.

The sun sure felt good as I lay back on a fallen tree, closed my eyes and started to drift off. When I thought I heard someone mumbling, my eyes popped open and I sat halfway up and drew my six-gun. I sat totally still, as I cocked my head in the direction it came from and then I cocked my Army Colt as well. Nothing! . . . Must've been in my head. I lay back and had started to drift off again, when I heard it once more. I got up and started walking quietly in the direction of the sound with my Colt .44 at the ready.

It was a little louder now and sounded like a chant, with the added sound of a small drum and rattle. As I approached the very peak of the low mountain I saw an old, thin Indian sitting on a flat rock beating a small drum. He faced the rising sun with his eyes closed, his chant carried off on the wind.

He spoke! "How! . . . Roy!" His eyes opened and he took in the sight of me standing there, my mouth open, a six-gun in my hand.

"You shoot old Indian?" he said in fair English.

I was flabbergasted. I hadn't made a sound while stalking him – and how in blazes did he know my name? I'd never seen him before in my life.

"What are you doing here?" I managed to mumble.

"Me pray to Great Spirit," the old man replied.

"How do you know my name?" I asked.

"Great Spirit spoke your name as I pray," he answered.

I looked the old Indian over as I holstered my shooting iron. He was just skin and bones. He must be starving up here without any way to get some game. Well, I wasn't one to refuse help to anyone in need so I asked him to join me for breakfast. Even though it hadn't been that long since I'd eaten.

We walked back to the field where I had turned out my mules. They were still grazing contentedly and hardly looked up. I soon had a fire going and cooked up some bacon and eggs. The old man ate like a stray dog and then held out his tin plate for more. While we were eating I asked the Indian what he had been praying for. He said he was praying for bacon and eggs because he was sick of rabbit and roots.

Then I asked him just how the Great Spirit knew my name? He told me that he probably overheard it in town when the storekeeper asked me where I was off to this time.

Well, I felt like I had been hornswaggled by this crafty old coot, so I just chuckled. The joke was on me.

We sat and talked half the morning as the sun climbed higher in the sky. His English was perfect, better'n mine. A couple of French missionaries had schooled him, so he spoke French and a little Swedish, too. He told me his name was "Black Cloud" and that he was a medicine man and could see the future. He could guide the thoughts of men and had much power.

I asked him what he was doing here so far from his people. He told me he was indeed far from his people and that he had been banned from his tribe by Chief Mad Bear, who thought the old Indian, was growing too powerful and might try to replace him as leader. The council told him not to return upon penalty of death.

So he had gone west to see where the sun slept

at night, but he was stopped by the big lake and could find no path around it. With sadness in his voice, he said he had left his people over thirty years ago and had been wandering ever since. I asked him if he had a squaw back in his homeland. He said yes, but that he was glad to get away from all the talk she made. He said he feared her more than the death threat.

"If you are so powerful, why don't you cast a spell on her?" I said.

The old man replied, as most men, he had no power over women! Then he looked me in the eye and told me I had been kind to him and we would meet again. If! . . . If I holed-up from the snow storm tonight and sheltered my mules from the blizzard for three days. I started to smile and laugh it off, but he looked at me with penetrating black eyes that seemed to bore into my thoughts. He was dead serious, so I decided I would humor him.

There wasn't a cloud in the sky. It was a great spring day and a blizzard was the last thing I'd bet on.

As we shook hands, he laid his left hand on top of mine, looked me in the eye and said, "Beware of blue eyes. They could be the death of you."

When we parted company, he handed me a little leather poke on a thong to wear around my neck to ward off evil spirits. I thanked him and waved goodbye and then the mules and I started once again down the trail.

I had a choice to make when I crossed the next

valley. One path was a little more roundabout and had a line cabin I could reach by sundown. The other one was much shorter and had more exposure to a north wind. Well, I must've been getting a little soft in the head because I chose the longer route, even though I was behind schedule.

When I was about a half mile from the cabin and the sun was low in the west, it suddenly got dark. A huge black cloud boiled over the ridge above me, bringing the smell of snow. Then a bone-chilling blast of wind hit me, knocking me back a step. I shivered from the cold – and from thinking about what the Indian had said.

The ferocity of the gust caused the forest litter to be swirled and hurled about, stinging man and beast alike. I broke into a quick trot and barked at the mules to keep up. The snow was piling up fast. Fortunately it took me only a few minutes to reach the line shack.

As I led each of the four mules into the lean-to, I removed their packs and built a partial wall with them to give the mules a little extra protection from the biting wind. Then I put a generous amount of oats in their feed bags and with their blankets on, they would do just fine.

With the mules fed, watered and set for the night, I entered the cabin. I had been there years before and was surprised to find everything in good shape. I shuttered all the window openings and then lit the oil lamp hanging from a rafter.

I checked the old potbellied stove. Bless the man

who was here last. He had laid a fire in the stove and all I had to do was light a taper from the lamp (always save a Lucifer if you can) and touch the tinder. I had a toasty fire going in no time and snow in the pot for coffee water. The wood-box to the right of the stove was overflowing, so I was in good shape for the night. Before I left, I'd have to fill the box and lay a fire for the next fellow. The "Code of the West" had to be obeyed: Always leave the camp better than you found it.

I sat on a wooden box enjoying, my evening pipe, contemplating the day's events – and what a strange day it had been. How could the weather change so fast? It had me puzzled. I had never seen anything like it in my . . . (let's see, this is 1873, minus 1833, equals) . . . about forty years. Well, I'll be. I'm getting to be an old-timer.

The ancient Indian had told me his name was "Black Cloud." *How fitting*, I mused. All night and for the next three days the wind howled, rattling the shutters and shaking the cabin. Snow sifted in every crack, making little white triangles. Twice each day, I checked on the girls and gave them oats. I also built a snow wall on the open side of the lean-to using fir branches and snow. The swirling wind filled in the rest.

Just as predicted by the old man, the storm lasted three days. On the fourth day, the sun broke out shining on three feet of snow. Travel was impossible for another three days, so I spent the time re-supplying the cabin with wood, filling the lantern and doing a few minor repairs.

*   *   *

Midway up the Rogue River Valley there is a tributary called the "Bogus River." It takes off to the north with a big mouth, but it's quickly reduced to a small creek within twenty miles. So it's all mouth and there's not much to it. That's why they call it "Bogus River." (They could have called it "Politician Creek" because that would have been more fitting.) It was a pleasant enough valley with some good grazing, a little bottom land and a few active mining claims up near the source.

My business was delivering supplies to the miners, but I also had a letter to deliver at Bill Boggs place when I passed there. They called him "Bully Bogus Billy." (But not to his face). He was meaner than a wolverine, slicker than slug snot, a thief and a liar. Those were his good points. He was the orneriest, cussingest critter ever unfortunately to be hatched on the face of the Earth. When he spoke, it was more like an eruption of smoke and fire. I swore I could see little bolts of lightening dancing between his pointy teeth. If I were to repeat his words they would burn holes in the air and scorch the pages of this book. (I'll translate his words here into less inflammatory language.)

I wasn't looking forward to dealing with this Jasper, because he had a reputation for picking on anybody smaller, weaker or kinder than he was. And that was just about everybody! There were rumors that he had murdered and robbed travelers, but nothing was ever proved.

The morning I was due to pass his place, I went

through my mail bag to make sure the letter was still there. That's when I noticed it was from the Oregon State Prison. Hum. . . .

A parcel of hound dogs covered the front porch and they put up a fuss when they caught my scent as I approached the cabin. The door banged open and a large man came out to see what all the commotion was about. He turned his head back towards the door and bellowed, "It's only Rogue River Roy." Then two more men came out. The last and largest I recognized as Billy Boggs. He yelled at the hounds to shut up and then turned his attention to me.

"Well, if it ain't old @#$%*&#@ Roy. Come on @#$%^&**&^%$#@ in and take a load off your @#$%^&* feet." (I cleaned that up a little.)

The air fairly crackled with each word he spoke. I really didn't want to visit with this grainy character. He made me real uncomfortable.

When I entered the house, I was surprised to find it quite spic and span. A thin, blue-eyed woman with blond hair pulled tightly to the back of her head nodded a welcome to me, but she was silent. Bogus Billy bellowed at her to fetch some coffee and cuffed her as he passed her to sit at the table. Then each of his boys cuffed her in turn as they also sat down. She didn't protest, but just kept silent as she served the steaming brew.

I took note of her with a sideways glance. She looked old for her years. Her rough hands smoothed her homespun dress as she waited their next command. She tried to stay out of reach of Bogus Billy as she went about her duties and flinched whenever the bully moved his hands. I wanted to say something in her behalf, but when you're a guest in another man's castle you can't interfere.

The letter I carried was addressed to "Mrs. Ellen Boggs." I reached in my mailbag and handed her the envelope, only to have it snatched away by Billy.

Her protest died on quivering lips as the bully ripped open the letter meant for her. I knew Boggs couldn't read (most bullies are ignorant). He wadded it into a ball and threw it out the window. Old Bully Boggs roared stop "@#$%^&* standing around here and get out and do your @#$%^&% chores," and then he cuffed her again as she headed out the door.

One of my mules started to beller – probably a hound-dog snapping at her heels. I thanked my host for the coffee and made my excuses. I was really eager to be on my way.

I was only a few hundred yards down the trail when Ellen, the Boggs' woman, stepped out of the brush and handed me a letter to post for her. I started to apologize for her husband's behavior and my inability to defend her (as a man should), but she interrupted me and said she was used to it and for me to "pay no never mind."

Mrs. Boggs asked me if the next time I had a letter for her would I just push it in the knot hole in the maple tree that stood behind her. I told her I would be happy to and I asked if there was anything else I could do for her. It was then that I noticed the crumpled letter in her fist. She must've retrieved it from the yard.

Ellen started to speak, but her chin began to quiver and she couldn't blink back the tears that welled up in her eyes. Her shoulders shook as she tried to stifle a sob. I couldn't help myself. I took her in my arms to comfort her – she was so helpless and brave. She held me tight until her sobbing stopped and she regained control.

Suddenly, I felt pressure on my back! The first thing I thought of was that Bully Boggs had caught me with his wife in my arms. This was a life or death situation! A vision of Black Cloud flashed before me, "Beware blue eyes. They could get you killed." I expected to hear the cocking of a gun at my back! Then I felt a little nudge. It was Ruby, my lead mule, pushing me. She was anxious to get on the trail and probably a little jealous of Ellen. I told her, "Easy girl – we'll be moving out shortly." Ellen gave me a strange look, but then she saw the mule behind me, and for the first time I saw her smile. It was beautiful. She took my hand and started to walk along with me, telling me the story of her life with Bully Boggs.

She had been widowed at the age of nineteen with a three-year-old son. A renegade Indian by the name of "Yellow Dog" had killed her husband and ran off their small herd of cattle. They had been trying to prove-up a homestead near Shoshone, Idaho and were struggling to make a success of their little ranch. Then that horrible renegade took it all away in one cruel morning. The death of her husband had left her stranded far out on the prairie in a remote little valley. It was a full month before anyone came out that way, but her luck didn't change, because it was Billy Boggs and his two sons, Billy Jr. and young Brutus. They were about seven and nine and already little copies of their disgusting father.

The Boggs had been traveling with a wagon train, but they had been asked to leave because Billy was just too ornery. He had picked on and humiliated every man smaller than himself. Finally, they had enough, got together and voted him and his boys off the wagon train. (He had virtually worked his wife to death – just left her on the prairie – didn't even have the decency to give her a Christian burial.)

When the bad-tempered Boggs came upon the forlorn widow, he loaded all her food and anything else he could find of value onto his wagon and then asked her if she wanted to come along. She had no choice, so she and young Eric left with him, hoping they could escape at the next town. But Bully Boggs always stopped outside of any settlement and took Ellen's young son with him when he went for supplies. She knew he would kill Eric if she ran off, so from that time on she became his virtual slave. That's how Ellen ended up on the Bogus River some fourteen years ago.

About six months ago the brothers had invited young Eric to go with them to pickup some cattle over by Medford. For years the bigger boys had done nothing but bully, torment and tease the lad. Now they wanted him to go with them on a cattle-buying drive. He said he didn't want to go, but Bully Boggs said, "You will @#$%^&* go, you @#$%@^&^B*&."

When the brothers came back, Eric wasn't with them. They said he'd run away over by Klamath Lake. Ellen said she thought it was for the best that Eric had struck out on his own, but it wasn't really like him to leave without saying goodbye.

About three months before, she had walked some ten miles to the general store at Illahe on the Rogue River to buy fifty pounds of flour. The store-keeper said a letter had been dropped off for her about a month earlier and he handed it to her. It was from her son. She ripped it open and read it right away. Eric was in Oregon State Prison and the lengthy letter told the whole story of how he got there.

When he and the brothers were over by Medford, the brothers had robbed a stage while Eric was back at camp watching the cattle they had just bought. When Sheriff Will Ketchem and his posse caught up to them, the brothers blamed the whole thing on Eric and even went to court as witnesses against him. Since it was his first offense, they only gave him five years, even though the money, rings and jewelry from the passengers were not recovered. (So, that explained the money, necklace, diamond stickpin and rings she had found in the boys' room when she did the laundry.)

"Those dirty @#$%&* scoundrels." She swore out loud for the first time in her life and the store-keeper and a lady customer looked at her, stunned.

"I'll need pen, ink and paper - now!" she ordered. She was a mother aroused, protecting her own. The proprietor jumped to her command and even offered his desk for her to use. She wrote three letters: a lengthy one to the Governor of Oregon, an informative one to Sheriff Ketchem (in which she described the loot she had found) and one to her son.

Ellen continued her story, telling me the letter she had just received was from her son. It said Sheriff Ketchem had investigated the hold-up and would be calling on her to recover the stolen loot and arrest the two men responsible. He had been contacted by Governor Peter DeFoxio and was advised of the situation.

I asked if there was anything I could do for her. In fact, I told her that she could come with me if she wanted. "I can take you to Grants Pass if you've a mind to." "Bully Boggs is a dangerous man, a known killer. It would be best if you left the scoundrel."

"Thanks anyway, but I have a plan," Ellen said, as she stepped off the trail and waved goodbye. She reached into her apron pocket and gave each mule a carrot as they passed by.

On the way back to the cabin she picked up some cascara bark that she had stripped the month before.

*   *   *

The shrill whistle of the Rogue River Queen broke the quiet of the evening as she came around Dead Man's Bend, heading for the landing on the

Bogus. The Queen could make it this far up the Rogue, but only in the spring and winter. She would tie up at the landing load her cargo and leave at eight o'clock the next morning.

The pieces of Ellen's plan were coming together. Early the next morning, she made a huge breakfast for Bully Boggs with lots of strong, cascara-enhanced coffee. She even flavored the sausage with the stimulating herb. About seven-thirty, after knocking Ellen about, the bully sat down at the table and ate a hardy meal. Junior and his brother were not at breakfast because they were on another cattle *buying* trip.

About ten minutes to eight, Bully Bogus Bill Boggs made a run for the outhouse, faster than he'd moved in twenty years. As he slammed the door, Ellen emerged from behind the noisy structure and turned the outside latch. Then she tied a one-inch rope around the little building and made a knot, called a "Moon House Bend." The other end was already looped around a big cleat on the stern of the River Queen.

At precisely eight o'clock, the Rogue River Queen castoff and gave a long blast of her shrill whistle. Her large side wheels began to churn the clear water. As the slack was pulled out of the rope, it twanged out of the river with a spray of water. Then the line tightened around the outhouse and yanked it off its site and skidded it into the river. The captain didn't hear the commotion over the sounds of the steam engine, as he looked downstream on his way to Gold Beach.

As Ellen watched the side-wheeler churning

down the Rogue towing the old outhouse around Dead Man's Bend, she thought to herself, *Free at last; free at last. Thank goodness I'm free at last!*

*   *   *

When Brutus and Junior came back with some rustled cattle the next day, Sheriff Will Ketchem was there to arrest them.

A few days later the Curry County Sheriff from Gold Beach, Pokey Smith, arrived to investigate the mysterious demise of the infamous bully, Billy Boggs. It was determined that the cattle-rustler, women-beater, kidnapper, killer, bully and all round bad guy had tied his boat to the Rogue River Queen to catch a free tow down river. He had seriously misjudged the seaworthiness of his craft – a very unusual design – and as a result he had caused his own passing. Case closed.

Eric arrived a month later with a pardon from Governor Peter DeFoxio and a letter of apology. Ellen and Eric ran the successful Bogus River Cattle Company for many happy years.

That ranch was a favorite place for me to stop-over because Ellen made the second best APPLE PIE in the whole Rogue River Valley.

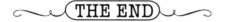

THE END

TALE THREE
LITTLE HOOVES
AND BIG FEET

Now, I think I have some of the smartest mules in the whole Rogue River Valley. No . . ! in the whole of Oregon. Actually, as I'm sworn to tell the truth, the "whole" truth, and nothing but the truth, then I reckon the "whole" world would be more like it. So, let me tell you a little story to prove my point.

First of all, you must know something about mules. If you breed a horse with a desert ass, you get a small mule with little hooves. The smaller the hooves, the more sure-footed the animal is. Look at mountain goats – if they had hooves as big as a horse's they would be falling down those mountains so often they would turn into valley sheep.

Another thing, mules are real proud of their small feet, especially the Jennies. If they're out in a pasture with horses, they always stand with their front hooves a little forward just to rub it in.

I had me four Jennies, rather than Jacks, because with those stubborn males you have to throw gravel in their ear to get them to mind. With the females, all you have to do is sweet talk 'em.

I think I've misled you a bit – this story isn't just about mules. It's about the most extraordinary critter ever discovered by mankind. It all happened one day awhile back when I was transporting some mining supplies and mail to the upper Rogue River Valley. Now, when I say "valley," I don't mean a gentle, grass-covered slope miles wide, ending in a mud-colored river that you can't tell the direction it's flowing. No sir. I mean shear rock walls and ridges that look like the business side of a crosscut saw. And water that's so clear, if it wasn't beaten to a white froth you wouldn't be able to see it. Now, you want to talk about flow! If you were lucky enough to survive falling in, you'd be six miles downstream by the time you came up for your first breath, but your clothes would be clean as a whistle.

I took my four favorite most sure-footed mules with me on this trip. The trail was cut into the face of a cliff and so narrow that it would make a mountain goat stop dead in its tracks and swallow hard.

Ruby was my lead mule. She was a little plumper than the others, so she was up front. If she could get through the narrow places they all could. That way you wouldn't be stuck with half your train on one side and half on the other. The next in line was Opal. She was the daredevil of the four and I have many tales to prove it. The third mule was Pearl. She was the smartest and she proved it time after

time. Last but least was Emerald the smallest bravest and my favorite. Yes, they were all gems in the
rough, every one.

It was the fourth day on the trail, just after
biscuits and coffee, when the girls came around. I
yelled "R-O-P-E!" and those mules lined up perfect.
R-uby, O-pal, P-earl, and E-merald were all lined up
in order and waiting for me to put their packs on.
Now, that's pretty smart and I never even trained 'em!
We were picking our way along a narrow trail about
three hundred feet above the river. As we came around
a bend I saw something on the path ahead. It looked
like a huge, dead bear. The closer I got, the bigger it
appeared and then it moaned! . . . Oh! Oh! This could
be big trouble! A wounded bear was nothing to trifle
with especially on a high narrow path. The only thing
to do was back on out quietly, very quietly!

I whispered "EPOR" – which is ROPE backwards
– and darned if those girls didn't just whirl around
and head back down the trail. It was a long way back
to a trail that would bypass this area so I figured I
best solve the problem. I told Em to stay put and
then I pulled my Winchester from the scabbard attached to her pack and started back up the path. As
I approached the huge bear lying on the trail, I noticed his big feet. They were not like any I had ever
seen on a grizzly. The critter moaned again and I froze.
With sweaty hands I flipped off the safety. As I took
aim I could feel my pulse pounding in my throat. Then
he turned his head and for the first time I saw those
large, blue eyes!

His dark brow was covered with sweat and he was shaking most violently. I could see both fear and pain in his eyes as he fought to stay awake. I advanced cautiously, my finger on the trigger, not taking any chances. Then I noticed the large splinter through his foot or paw or whatever it was called. Anyway, it was swollen twice the size of the other one - and that was sizable.

I knelt beside him and discovered he had just passed out. I cautiously touched his sloping forehead and found it hotter than a frying pan. I figured as long as he was unconscious I might as well cut that chunk of wood out. There was a small overhang a couple of hundred feet back down the trail where I could build a fire to heat up my Bowie knife. The only problem was to get this huge critter back to the sheltered area. I called "Em! Em! Come on girl!"

She came around the bend in a few minutes and just walked right up to me without even a blink. Now, that's what I call spunk! Most animals would have high-tailed it out of there, but not old Emerald. She was my brave girl and I told her so. I rigged up a drag, hitched it to my favorite mule. She backed up to the overhang, nice as you please.

Well, I got a fire going and had the splinter out before that hairy monster even knew what was happening. It took about two days of doctoring and feeding him grub till he was on the mend. It was then I found out they were vegetable eaters like dandelions and such. He wouldn't eat bacon, jerky or anything good.

While he was still stoved-up, I backtracked his trail and discovered what most-likely happened. He was traveling through a logged-off area and had vaulted over a log. His foot came down on a fresh-cut stump that had all those jagged spines on it. The wood broke off, his foot got infected and then he got sick with a fever. That's when I found him.

The first time he was able to stand up I was frightened all over again. This Jasper was so tall that it hurt my neck to look up at him. I'll bet he must've weighed over four hundred pounds. While we were sitting around the fire, he would hand me whatever I was planning to motion him for and I somehow figured out he could read my mind. *So that's how they did it.* When you're out walking in the woods and you hear something behind you and turn around, he's already hiding. He reads your mind and he knows you are going to look back.

"Well, I'll be!" I said aloud. For the first time I saw him smile! Those teeth of his were huge. I tried to return the smile, but I was just too scared!

We parted company because he was ready to travel and I had mail and goods to deliver to people who were waiting for 'em. I'd like to tell you this was the end of my encounter with that big-footed critter, but it wasn't.

The land gradually leveled out as we started into ranch country. I and the girls would soon be at the Widow Wilson's spread and my mouth started to water thinking about it.

As always, she was happy to see me. She even

had carrots for my mules. I handed her a letter from her middle daughter who lived in Grants Pass and she could hardly wait to read it. She cried when she came to the part about her new grandson and told me everything was just fine.

Now we come to what I'd been waiting for! The widow invited me in for coffee and "APPLE PIE!" This wasn't just Apple Pie – this was "APPLE PIE!" The best pie I had ever tasted. Why, sometimes I would go forty miles out of my way for a single slice of Widow Wilson's Apple Pie. As usual, I raved about her pie, because whenever I did she would send me on my way with a big piece to have for breakfast on the trail.

Well, I'd gone about ten miles from the widow's ranch when I felt like someone was watching me. Sure enough that old hairy monster dropped out of a fir tree right in front of me. Scared the whey out of me! He just smiled and stood there, all eight feet of him. It took a full five minutes before I could stop shaking long enough to sign him a hello.

This was a good place to camp for the night, so I signed him my intentions. He smiled and I shuddered at the sight of those teeth. I built a small fire after putting the mules out to graze and then lay back against a tree to enjoy the fire. Then the darndest thing happened. Big foot reached into his pocket . . . and pulled out an apple! I was flabbergasted! He saw me looking at him really weird and he shyly pulled another apple out of his pocket and then buttoned it up with his belly button. I was dumbfounded. These critters were like possums or kangaroos they had pouches (with buttons even). He offered me the apple, but I refused because I was eating a little jerky. Later, I found out that apples are the favorite food of these mysterious forest dwellers.

We spent an uneventful night and that's unusual around here. The next morning, I made the biggest mistake of my life! I shared my "APPLE PIE" with old blue eyes! It was like giving a stray dog a big juicy steak. Now this guy was just too big to chase away with a stick, so I would have to think of some other way to get rid of him. The big feller disappeared as I was breaking camp and I thought that would be the last of him.

When the girls came around from their foraging they were a little skittish, having had a monster in camp and all. When I yelled "ROPE!" they all lined up and were as good as gold.

Well, I'd been on the trail for only a few minutes when that big galoot dropped out of a pine tree in front of me and scared me half to death, again! I think it amused him to see me draw my Colt, then freeze in my fighting crouch with a terrified look on my face. He looked like he was putting on a little weight. Then he pulled an apple out of his pouch. He must've had a bushel of 'em! He offered me one and I nodded my head in thanks. Then he walked down the mule train giving each girl an apple in turn. "You can steal a mule's heart with an apple a day." [An old Johnny Chapman saying.]

That critter must've doubled back to the Wilson ranch and raided the apple orchard, but he wasn't gone over a half hour. It was over twenty miles away and he had to do the picking too. I confess I can't do the ciphering, but that Bigfoot must've been traveling faster than an antelope with its tail on fire and a bee in its ear.

As things would have it I traveled the trails dropping off supplies and mail for another two weeks. Every now and again I'd catch a glimpse of the scruffy critter as he followed along. He would show up at sundown and sleep near the fire that he didn't fear.

We passed a farmer's field one day and that night the big guy showed up with a pocket full of summer squash. He'd just take one and slam it on a rock, then eat the pieces, seeds and all. After running around with squash in his belly-bag a couple three days, they began to get a little "ripe." When he emptied his pouch near the fire, I said "Whew, such squash!" I had to move the fire about fifty yards down the trail.

Then it came to me I hadn't named him yet. (I had just called him "big fella.") I decided to call him "Such Squash," and I guess the name stuck.

*   *   *

To make a short story long, at the end of the circuit we ended up at a friend's place on the lower Rogue River. Rupert and Ruth always welcomed me with kindness and they really liked the little gifts I brought them from town. Ruth was the second best Apple Pie maker in the Rogue Valley, a fact that never crossed my lips, especially if I still expected to eat some more of her pie.

I thought maybe I was playing a dirty trick on them by leading old Such into their neck of the woods, but what could I do? It wasn't as if I had any control over this big galoot.

As luck would have it Ruth had just baked two Apple Pies. Now, the only thing better than one hot Apple Pie is two hot Apple Pies. I swear, the aroma drifting off those pies cooling on the windowsill could have drawn a grizzly bear out of a snug cave in the middle of a blizzard. I could just feel that flaky crust melting on my tongue and those scrumptious apples covered my taste buds with tantalizing delight . . . ummm! I was brought back to reality by a high-pitched whistle far off in the woods. Someone else had got the drift also.

Dinner was really outstanding with venison stew and baking powder biscuits, except for the scream that followed. It was Ruth standing at the window looking out into the night frozen with terror. Her face was white and her jaw was moving without a sound heard. Rupert said, "What in the world is it?"

She was barely able to point out the window and stammer "gone." We both looked out into the blackness and saw nothing. I looked down and of course one pie was gone. I told them I would explain everything over a cup of coffee.

We returned to the table and Ruth poured the coffee with shaky hands. They sat down to listen intently as I began to tell my incredible story. I shouted

"No!" ... and jumped up and made a dash for the window. I grabbed the remaining pie and returned to the table with a triumphant look on my face.

Rupert had had enough, "Confound it Roy, what in the blue blazes is going on?"

I knew I had better start talking fast. So I began my story back when I thought I saw a bear wounded on the trail up till we sat down at the table. They just sat there dumbfounded, shaking their heads in disbelief. Ruth accused me of playing a trick on her as I had done many times in the past.

The longer I talked the more they thought I was telling another tall tale. It's really difficult to tell someone an incredible story that's absolutely the truth, the whole truth and nothing but the truth. (Sound familiar?) Now, I must admit – being honest and almost truthful – that in the past once or maybe thrice, I had been misunderstood or not heard quite right while narrating some story. In addition facts sometime have to be . . . adjusted . . . or . . . interpreted to better understand the circumstances of the tale . . . err . . . narration.

My defense was crumbling fast and I felt like I was diggin' myself in deeper and deeper. Then Rupert accused me of taking the Apple Pie to eat later. [The image of old Squash out there eating that whole pie did appeal to me.] I was beginning to feel guilty and saddened to hear the accusations. Then the most wonderful, terrible thing happened. Such Squash put his head in the open window and smiled! There was still a little pie crust on those horrible teeth.

Their old house was built on a small hill – with the front being lower than the back. So the bottom of the kitchen window was about six feet off the ground. Such Squash was standing there with his elbows resting on the windowsill, a big smile and a very guilty look on his face. I caught Ruth as she screamed her way into oblivion and fell backwards into my arms. Rupe stood there speechless his eyes frozen wide open. The good thing was they finally believed me. The bad thing was they were very angry with me because I didn't warn them about the monster.

THE END

Not really. This is just the beginning of a whole bunch of stories about how Old Blue Eyes livened up livin' on the Rogue.

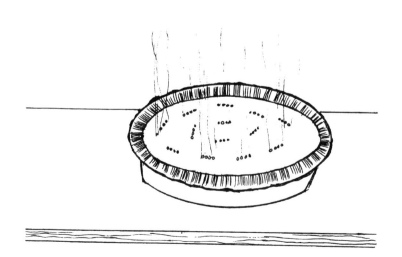

TALE FOUR
BIG CAT,
BIG TEETH

I've seen some mighty huge fish in my time on the Rogue River and I've seen some hellacious big bears, but I ain't never seen the likes of the cougar I'm gonna to tell you about. I should have turned the mule train around, right when I came upon those monster tracks. I had left town early that morning with my four best mules, Ruby, Opal, Pearl and Emerald – of course, every one was a gem. I had some grub to deliver to an outfit of miners up on the Rogue River.

It was getting late in the day and a fine spring day it had been. There was pale, new greenery everywhere. The trail was still a little damp under the overhanging fir trees, with a few mud puddles here and there. I casually noticed one puddle that was shaped like a huge cat track – it was big and must've been a coincidence, of course. Then I saw another . . . ! Then another . . . ! They were real. The muddy water was still swirling in 'em.

I had my Colt .44 in my hand, but I didn't even remember drawing it. The hair on the back of my neck rose up like the quills on a porcupine. I called for the girls to close up. This was a bad situation - there was too much cover to hide in.

These were the biggest cat tracks I had ever seen, bigger than I could even imagine. They must've been a foot across! That meant the critter that made them must weigh at least eight hundred pounds – if it weighed an ounce. This thing would have to be over ten feet long, not including its tail! A mountain lion that big could eat a whole mule for supper and have me for dessert.

I didn't have time to get any scareder than I already was, because with an ear splitting scream, the huge cat leaped out of the brush and landed right on Emerald's pack, driving her to her knees.

Emerald was packing forty slabs of smoked bacon for the miners and the scent must've driven that big cat wild. He bit right through the canvas and didn't even touch the terrified mule. The other three mules came roaring by me in a wild-eyed blur. I dove off the trail and rolled head-over-heels down the slope. When I stopped, all I could hear was that mule braying with all her might. I scrambled back up the slope like a wild man, only to discover I had lost my Colt in the fall. My Marlin rifle was on the lead mule's pack and she was long gone up the trail.

Emerald was trying to struggle to her feet, but the cat was too big for her. I had to help her! I grabbed a large stick and started beating the monster cat on the head. He was so engrossed in eating the bacon that it took about five whacks to get his attention. Then he turned his massive head and screamed at me, as if that would be enough to scare me off.

It was more than enough, but I was so darned scared I got mad that I picked up a bigger stick and really started to wale on his noggin. His ten-inch teeth flashed in a shaft of sunlight and it wasn't a smile, as he once again looked at the puny creature that was interrupting his meal. I bonked him on the nose and then he really got mad. He took a swipe at me and shredded the stick and then he leaped towards me as the mule kicked out. She caught him on the side of the head – it hardly fazed him, but it was enough to make him miss me.

It was then that I realized I was in trouble. I knew I couldn't out run him, so I jumped behind a big fir tree, but he saw me and started after me. Now, that tree was about twenty-five feet around at the base and I started running around it as fast as I could with that mountain lion on my tail. Actually, I was on his tail. I was running for all I was worth and so was he. His tail was about eight feet long and it kept getting in my face so I grabbed on to it. I heard a howl from somewhere behind or ahead of me and then we really started moving. I couldn't keep up, so I started sliding along behind. Soon my boots started to smoke and my soles were getting hot and real thin. Lucky for me, one of those slabs of bacon was by the tree, so I just jumped on and went bouncing along, slicker'n slug snot, behind that wild cougar.

The slab of smoked bacon started to get a little warm after about a hundred times around that tree. Then it started to smoke a little; then it started to sizzle; and then it started to smell real good. Boy, talk about mixed emotions – I was scared, mad, tired, hungry and getting' real dizzy.

We must've circled that tree a thousand times, when I thought I saw Black Cloud standing on the trail watching. "Roy, I . . . . never seen anyone . . . . cook bacon like that before," he said.

The mountain lion's tail must've been stretching, because he was catching up with me! He was snapping at my backside. This situation was getting serious! I yelled at Black Cloud, "Are you gonna . . . . do something . . . . or are you . . . . just gonna . . . . stand there?"

"Will you give me . . . . your secret biscuit recipe, Roy?" said the old Indian.

"Yes, yes, yes . . . . anything, confound it, just hurry."

The cat stumbled and we ended up in a big heap with me on top! Black Cloud grabbed the bacon first and then gave me a hand up. I just kept spinning and spinning. I couldn't stand up. He started spinning me in the opposite direction. After about half an hour things started to slow down and I was back to normal, or as normal as I could get. The first thing Black Cloud said was, "Looks like I saved your bacon again Roy."

He started to build a fire, right on the trail. I stared at him quizzically and he said, "So you can show me how to make your famous biscuits."

"Are you going to hold me to that?" I said.

"I could have asked for your rifle and your Army Colt as well. You got off easy Roy."

He was right. I was lucky to be alive. Then he added, "I was going to save you anyway Roy, 'cause the bacon was starting to burn."

I wondered if he had done something to bring down the monster. "What did you do to the cougar? Cast one of your famous spells on him?"

"No, no, nothing like that. It's just that he lost so much weight chasing you around that tree that his skin got loose and he tripped on it. Then he stumbled, fell, and broke his neck, poor kitty." He gave me a big smile. "Now let's have some bacon 'n' biscuits."

THE END

TALE FIVE
MAGNETIC
MOUNTAIN

Now, the first thing that gave me a clue that there was something strange going on in this part of the Rogue River Valley was when my new compass just didn't act quite right. Don't get me wrong I'm no tender-foot and a real mountain man never used a compass in his whole life and wouldn't get caught dead with one.

There was this federal guy who came through and he was lost. He wanted me to make a map of the Rogue Valley and it had to have a "North'" on it. So being the kind person I am, I agreed to help him if he would give me a compass for the purpose of marking on the map. Of course, the ten dollars in gold he offered also helped! His name was Lewis N. Clark and he was from back east somewhere, back where they really didn't have a "great outdoors."

He was a decent enough fellow and the men he had with him were passable, but he had this here problem with some kinda "Government Pay Master," who thought he was two people instead of one. They was paying twice what he was worth. Captain Clark tried to straighten it out, but the government wouldn't admit they had made a mistake and they kept on insisting he was two people. I sometimes wonder how long they would try to cover up an error like that. *As if the government would try to cover up anything!* Oh well, I'm drifting a little, so I best get back to my story.

I was making a map of the middle part of the Rogue River, when I noticed the compass needle kept pointing at this one particular mountain – no matter what side of the mountain I was standing on. Now, I was familiar with this area and had been through here many times, but never having had a compass before, I did not know about this here defugalltee.

There was a gnarly snag that must've been four hundred feet high growing right on top. In the past, I had always called it *Snag Mountain.* One peculiar thing was that the top of this old tree must've been hit by lightning when it was half-growed, because it branched out in two directions at a point about a hundred feet from the top. It looked like a huge "Y" in the sky. That old Indian, Black Cloud, had warned me to never go near this mountain because it was the home of an evil spirit. I've never been one to scoff at Indian accounts or belittle their beliefs in the "Great White Spirit." More than once I've heeded a warnin' that saved my bacon. Nevertheless, I had to make that map.

I had two of my pack mules with me on this trip, old Rose and Evelyn. Normally, I never hobble my pack animals at night and they were always happy to stay right around camp. But this night was different. Along about midnight, after the fire had died down and was just a red glow in the darkness, I heard a women scream! It took me a couple seconds to wake up and, of course, I realized it was a mountain lion looking for supper. Mule must've been on the menu, because Rose was putting up quite a fuss. I could hear her crashing through the brush, trying to escape those deadly claws.

My Colt .44 was handy and I fired five shots in the air, hoping the noise might scare the predator away. Then I slipped on my boots, grabbed my Marlin .30.30, lit the lantern, and took off towards the sound of the breaking brush.

This was an eerie place and everything felt strange. Not the best place to be on a coal black night. But when you have a poor dumb beast in your care it's up to you to protect her.

I'll bet I hadn't gone over a hundred paces when there in the lantern light was that big old catamount. He had Rose cornered against a rock outcrop and was about to spring when he suddenly fell over dead . . . *What in green lighting was going on!*

I approached him cautiously and nudged him with the barrel of my rifle. Yep, he was stone dead. Then I noticed the four holes in the top of his head. Darned if the rounds I had fired in the air to scare him off hadn't come down right on his noggin. Some would say it was lucky shooting, but if it had been lucky, all five bullets would have nailed that critter.

Old Rose was too nervous to bring back to camp right then, so I thought I'd skin out the big cougar while I was waiting for her to calm down. When I hung that lantern on a tree branch to work by it didn't hang straight down, the bottom kinda swung towards the mountain. Now, what did that mean?

When I was done with my work, I looked around and darned if that blasted mule hadn't wandered off up the mountain. I wasn't about to go traipsing around in my red Union suit at night, so I gathered my caboodle and headed for camp to make some hotcakes and bacon and wait for daylight to find my mule.

In the morning I gave Evelyn some oats and then hobbled her before I took off up the mountain in search of Rose. I followed her tracks and the broken brush for about an hour. I could see that tall snag and it looked like Rose was making a bee line right for it. This really had me puzzled because she had never wandered off before. I gave a whistle and she answered with a loud bellow. Then I saw her. She was standing with her nose stuck to a boulder. What in the world was going on?

As I approached the cabin-sized rock, I saw an old rifle stuck to the side of it – also a frying pan, a horseshoe, a knife, an ax, and a pistol. There was all kinds of stuff stuck to that rock.

Then I felt myself being drawn towards the strange rock. I had a firm grip on my rifle, but it was being drawn to that big boulder as if by magic. My knife just flew out of the scabbard on my belt and stuck flat against it. The hair on the back of my neck stuck up like the feathers on an excited tom turkey – this was surely an unusual place!

Then it came to me what this thing was . . . it was a meteorite . . . like the North Pole: a magnet! That's what it was, a darn magnet. I looked up and saw that old snag. It must've been hit by the meteor. The meteor knocked the top of that tree clean off. Well, I'll be darned! The mystery was solved, but now I had to figure out how to get all my gear away from the attraction of the big rock.

Evidently old Rose had felt the gentle pull on her bridle and just followed it right to the meteor. I removed her bit and everything else that was metal and led her to a spot about fifty feet away and tied her to a tree. Next, I rigged up a kinda harness and used my ropin' line to pull each one of the metal objects off'n that big chunk of trouble.

Some of the stuff was rusty, but some was usable, so all in all it was a good trip. It was really just another typical day on the Rogue River.

THE END

TALE SIX
THE GREAT
SAWMILL FIRE

The great sawmill fire of 1888 happened in Coos Bay, Oregon on a windy October night. It had been a mild, dry fall and everyone was lulled into a false sense of security. Oly Olson was working at the brand new Big Bear Sawmill which was in its first month of operation. It was a great job, with all new equipment and good wages. Oly was making over twenty-five cents an hour and saving all the money he could manage. Before long, he would be able to send for his sweetheart, Mary, who was living at her folks' ranch on the Rogue River, about twenty miles up from Gold Beach, Oregon. The sooner he saved enough money the sooner they could be married. Oly volunteered for the graveyard shift to hurry things along – it paid an extra five cents an hour.

The new mill was built by Sawbucks R. Moneymaker the Third, a local banker and politician. The trees in Oregon were so large that a special mill was needed to handle the huge logs. The Big Bear Mill was just the ticket, everything about it was huge. It had the two biggest head saws in the world – over thirty feet across. One was mounted as a top saw; the other as the base saw. A tree twenty feet across was no match for these immense spinning blades. It had the largest steam carriage ever built to feed logs to the giant saws. Then came the boiler-house or steam-plant. It was fed hog fuel at the rate of a ton a minute. The smokestack was so tall that it was above the clouds most of the time.

Oly worked in the steam-plant as the lead fireman, adjusting the speed of the hog fuel chain to maintain the correct steam pressure. One night the outside temperature started to fall slowly at first, but when the wind picked up, it carried the smell of whale-oil lamps and cooking polar bear (not a good sign). The night crew was all snug and smug inside the warm boiler-house and didn't realize the danger. When the first slammer hit the building, everything shook violently. (A slammer is a wind gust within a wind gust; quite common on the South Coast of Oregon.) The temperature fell so fast it sheared off the bolts holding up the thermometer at the front gate. The guard spat a plug of tobacco at a stray cat and it froze in midair and then knocked the unfortunate critter unconscious. The log pond froze solid in seconds trapping all the logs. Strange things were happening all over the mill.

Meanwhile, back at the boiler-house the door burst open! Wind and cold came in with a bundled-

up man. When he took off his scarf, everyone could
see it was Sawbucks R. Moneymaker, himself! He
began to shout and give orders left and right! Get
that pressure up . . . ! More hog fuel . . . ! Start the
gang saws . . .! Get all the steam lines going . . . !
We're going to freeze up and lose the mill!

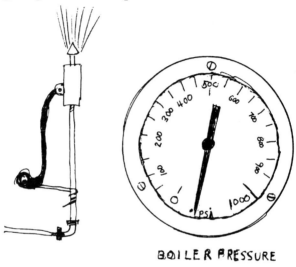

BOILER PRESSURE

The danger now became apparent to everyone.
The steam and condensation lines would all freeze
and burst because the new mill hadn't been insu-
lated yet. The wind was shaking the steam-plant con-
tinually and it was now forty degrees below zero. The
main boiler was drawing in fuel like a ten-year-old
boy eating candy. Everything began to glow red around
the enormous fire box and the roar was deafening.
The pressure gauges were "pegged out." Then the
safety valves began to pop off. Suddenly, a pressure
gauge blew, showering the fire-deck with glass. A
shrill whistle of steam added to the din!

"Wire the pop-off on those safety valves down!" said Mr. Moneymaker.

The doors on the fire box became white hot and started to bow-in – with a snap and a loud pop, they were sucked into the raging inferno. The hog-fuel began to be drawn in by the tremendous vacuum – the boiler was feeding itself! The worst had happened: a runaway boiler. A lunch pail on a nearby bench flew across the room and disappeared into the fire. The bench it had been on followed.

Everything that wasn't nailed down or bolted to the floor was drawn into the all-consuming mouth. The workmen began to desert the fire-deck, making a run for the door. When they opened it, the door was sucked off its hinges and entered the inferno. It was gone in an instant.

"Come back, you cowards," shouted Sawbucks. He was stretched out horizontal, hanging on to a post like a flag at half-mast.

First his boots were sucked off and then his suspenders stretched out almost twenty feet. They broke with a loud twang! His pants flew up the chimney like they had a mind of their own. He just whipped there in the suction wearing only his bright red Union suit (although he wasn't a Union man). At last, he could hold on no longer. He lost his grip, flew the length of the fire-deck and entered the furnace in a golden flash. (He would have liked the part about the "golden flash," being a rich man and all.)

Oly managed to get outside and head south with the wind, barely escaping with his life.

Millions of board feet of cut lumber from the drying stacks were drawn across the yard and consumed in the conflagration.

Everything in town that wasn't tied down came rolling down the hills, drawn to the huge self-feeding fire. All the toys left outside by careless children were gone with the wind in a puff of smoke.

The town was picked clean as a whistle.

Then the worst happened: the main saw building burst into flames, but instead of the smoke and fire going straight up, it was drawn through the fire box and up through the tall smoke stack. The noise it made was like a boom of thunder that just seemed to go on forever.

Like a huge wheel, the main saw blade came rolling out of the inferno, heading towards the boiler-house. The smokestack itself was starting to glow red! It was like a huge Roman candle, shooting sparks five miles into the night sky. It would have been a beautiful sight if it wasn't so deadly.

When the huge saw blade reached the bottom of the stack, there was a pause and then a tremendous explosion as the huge disc was blasted far, far above, into the stormy night.

*   *   *

About three weeks later, Rogue River Roy was on his mail route delivering goods and letters to all his friends and customers along the mighty Rogue River. His next stop was the Morgan Ranch, a nice spread nestled in a small valley. Old Man Morgan was a real tough and rough rancher, a good friend, and a bad enemy. He and Roy went back a long ways – they had even courted the same gal, who was now Mrs. Morgan.

There was a letter for Morgan's oldest daughter, Mary. She was engaged to a young fellow up in Coos Bay and this one was from him.

They were all seated on the front porch having coffee, except Mary, who was in her room reading her letter. She came bursting out of the front door with an anguished cry. "The mill burned down. Now I'll never get married." She began to sob uncontrollably.

Her mother took the letter from Mary's hand, because Mary could not continue reading with her tear-filled eyes.

"Oh! . . . Listen to this," and she went on to finish Oly's description of the Great Sawmill Fire of Coos Bay.

Just then a shadow passed across the porch and they all looked up to see a small round object falling out of the sky. It became larger and larger, until they could see it might be one of those huge saw blades from the mill.

Morgan became alarmed. "We better watch to see where this here thing is going to land. It could flatten the house if it comes down wrong."

As luck would have it, the object landed with a loud metallic bong right on top of a tall fir tree! The mounting hole of the saw stripped the branches off the tree as it slid down the trunk, slowing its descent.

Near the center of the giant blade stood a figure dressed in bright red long johns with a lunch-box in his hand. He jumped off the huge saw blade and started to shout and give orders. They all knew instantly that it was Sawbucks R. Moneymaker, The Third.

Mrs. Morgan said, "My word" when she saw the red clad figure. Then she headed for the house to get something decent for the poor man to put on.

Mr. Morgan walked up to Sawbucks and when he continued to shout orders, Morgan picked him up, held him eyeball to eyeball and said, "You're trespassing, mister and if you don't want to get shot up, shut up!"

Mr. Moneymaker thought about his available options and decided to become a most humble guest. After a few days rest and some good home cooking, he left for California. I heard he became governor the next year.

The good news is that Oly went into the charcoal business and made a fortune. He and Mary got married and they moved to Olympia, Washington, where he opened a brewery and they lived happily ever after.

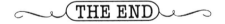

THE END

Remember the gigantic saw blade,
because you'll find it another story.

TALE SEVEN
THE ROGUE RIVER'S
FIRST LAUNDRY-MATIC

I was always looking to make an honest dollar whenever I saw the opportunity. It so happened I was hauling supplies to a mining camp on the Rogue and was crossing the river with my mule train about a mile from there. A rattlesnake went swimming by with a frog in his mouth. It startled me and caused me to step into a hole. I lost my balance and went under. Well, sir, that old river grabbed me and whipped me downstream three miles before I came up for my first breath.

I came up sputtering and gasping for air and boy, was I mad. Really mad! I was so steamed that my clothes dried within minutes. Here I was, miles downstream  from my mules.

But, then, when I looked at my clothes, I realized they were sparkling clean and so was I. Even my long-johns were white, including the trap-door. That gave me an Idea and I headed back overland to the mule train to put my plan into action.

I got to the miner's diggings and was paid for my goods and then I started to work on my plan. First, I built a little shack that hung right out over the river. I made a sign and nailed it to the front door. The sign read, "FREE BATH" and "CLOTHES WASHED, TEN CENTS."

It wasn't long till I had a long line of crusty miners waiting and eager to spend a little gold to get clean again. I spied my good friend and old partner Engine Joe waiting in line and I asked him how the digging was going. Joe said he had moved a lot of gravel, but he weren't having as much luck as some. I told him about my plan and soon Joe was headed downstream with the four mules from my pack train.

The first customer – they were customers now, not miners – walked the plank to the shanty and emptied his pockets into the little box provided then went inside.

As each customer walked in, the whole floor tilted and dumped the surprised man into the raging river. In a few short seconds, the miner would surface miles downstream right at "Sucker Bar," where Engine Joe snagged him with a big salmon net and hauled him out.

Most of the miners weren't too happy at first, sputtering and all, but when Joe pointed out how clean their duds were and then sprayed them with some lilac water, they simmered down.

They did start to get a little riled when they realized they were miles downstream from their claims, but then Joe pointed to the mules. "It'll only cost you a dime to ride back upriver to the camp, payable when you get there." Some of them started to get angry, but when they took a good look at the size of Joe, they calmed down and left quietly.

By the way, I forgot to tell you about Joe. The reason they called him Engine was because he was six feet, seven inches tall, weighed three hundred pounds of solid muscle, was strong as a steam engine, and black as boiler smoke. He was so strong he could pick himself up and then hold himself out at arms' length! A good friend and a bad foe.

Meanwhile, back at camp, business slowed down as I ran out of miners (we sure didn't get any repeat customers). Well, now you know where the expression "taken to the cleaners" came from. If you take care of all your big problems all your small ones will be miner.

THE END

TALE EIGHT
BIG VALLEY

I was up early and on the trail before dawn with my four pack mules. Ruby up front, Opal next, third in line was Pearl and last but not least was little Emerald. She was the smallest and bravest of the pack. We were headed down the Rogue River Valley on our way back to town. Now, when I say valley, it's not what the flatland foreigners call a valley, which is usually just a slump in the ground with a brown mudhole meandering through it. No sir! This was a rip-roaring, white-water, beat to froth, and honest to goodness raging river with banks of solid rock a thousand feet high and jagged as a grizzly's yawn in spring.

I could feel the warmth of the sun on my neck as it broke over the ridge behind me and I saw my long shadow contrasting against the trail ahead. The trail was steep and narrow, but the mules handled it with ease. The smell of evergreens wafted up the cliff from the trees far below. It was a great day to be alive.

As I came around a bend, the sunlight reflected off of something brilliantly shining on the cliff below the trail. Well, this was to be investigated – maybe someone had lost a polished knife or even a coin. I marked the spot in my mind by a small tree growing out of the cliff by the trail.

When I got there, I went down on all fours and peered over the edge. Well, darned if it didn't look like a pocket of GOLD!   The rain and a little slide had exposed a "glory hole," a patch of nuggets that had been deposited thousands of years ago.

The gold ore was a little out of reach, so with shaking hands I tied my ankles to that little fir tree across the trail. Then I lowered myself till the gold was within my grasp. My heart was pounding in my throat – because of the gold, not hanging upside down by my ankles a thousand feet above the raging Rogue River. I began stuffing gold into my leather pouch. It's really hard to not get a little greedy when it's just there for the taking. I kept stuffing and stuffing, till soon I must've had fifty pounds in my poke. When I started to pull myself up, I heard a loud snap! I froze and started to untie the pouch, but it was too late. That little tree broke in-two and I felt myself falling towards the river a thousand feet below. Three-hundred-foot tall trees looked like saplings as they rushed up to meet me.

Now, I've been in some tight places in my life. I once had a grizzly bear rip a heel off my boot and I've had a cougar on my back. I've been snake-bit, kicked, clawed, shot, stabbed, and even had my hair mussed

up once. Why, I've seen floods, earthquakes, torna-
does, bandits, war and that was all before I was six
years old!

I was usually able to think my way out of situ-
ations like this, but here I was, falling a thousand
feet to my sure death. Nothing could save me. My
last thought was *would my mules be all right without
me?*

Suddenly, a large shadow passed across me and
giant talons gripped the little tree I was hanging from.
It was the biggest Bald Eagle I had ever seen. I knew
in a flash those tall tales the old muleskinner told
were true. Old "H. J." had told stories about Big
Valley, where everything was gigantic, and no one
believed him. *Well, I'll be,* I said to myself.

The bird was over thirty feet across, with talons like boat anchors. He must've been out gathering
branches to add to his nest and that's where we were
heading. Evidently, the giant eagle hadn't seen me
dangling below the little fir tree. When he dropped
the tree (and me) into his nest, which was located on
a huge redwood growing high on the mountain, I
managed to scurry under the nest undetected.

I waited quietly until he had left in search of
more branches. Then I climbed into the nest and
looked around. There were two gigantic white eggs
warming in the morning sun. I put my ear against
one of them and heard thumping and scratching – I
was about to have company! I had to do something
real fast or I was going to be lunch.

I looked over the side – it must've been a thousand feet to the valley floor. What a predicament!

Several huge feathers were lying loose in the nest. I gathered the three biggest ones, pulled out my trusty Bowie knife, and set to work. I cut the end off of one feather and hollowed it out and inserted the other one in the hollowed end. It made a kinda wing. Then I twisted it till both faced up. I started to cut a hole through both feathers where they joined. Next, I pushed the third feather through both feathers to make a tail. I used the piece of rope from my ankles to tie it all together.

I really didn't have much of a choice as to whether to jump out of the giant redwood tree with this contraption or not. I was a goner if I stayed, so I just climbed up to the edge of the nest and launched myself into the morning breeze. *When you have to do something, just go ahead and do it.*

The feeling of falling free, spinning like a maple seed, is not my idea of a good time. I must've fallen three hundred feet before I shifted my weight and found I had a little bit of control.

As I was descending, I saw a mosquito fly by with a grizzly bear impaled on his beak. He hovered around me, but he must've figured I wasn't worth his trouble and so he flew off.

I knew for sure if I landed in Big Valley it would be the end of me, so I shifted my weight a little and managed to head south. The leather pouch filled with gold was still around my neck. I had forgotten all about it – what with trying to stay alive and all. If I was going to glide out of here, I was going to have to get rid of some weight. The gold had to go! I managed to save two nuggets, but the rest flashed in the sunlight as they fell to the earth below.

I was in familiar territory now and could see the trail I had been traveling on. A green meadow appeared and there were my girls grazing away. I shifted a little and headed towards them as best I could. I was getting the *hang of this gliding* and thought I was pretty good at it. A sudden gust of wind blew me a short distance away from the meadow. I crashed into a stand of saplings. I had never been so happy to be on solid ground in all my life. I bent over to kiss Mother Earth and found out I had knocked out my two front teeth.

I went to the dentist in Gold Beach when I got back to town, Dr. W. E. Pullum. Guess what it cost? Yep, two gold nuggets to have a couple of teeth made. Well, it wasn't all bad having them two front teeth replaced with gold. They saved my life that very next spring, but that's another story.

THE END

TALE NINE
FUNNY BONE
STEW

It was the end of a long hard day on the trail up the Rogue River and we had covered nearly thirty miles of rough Oregon country. The sun had just dipped below the jagged mountains and it was time to make camp for the night.

Engine Joe and I were hauling some mining gear up-country using my eight mules. We went back a long ways together – we were boys in Missouri and fought in the Civil War, but not on the same side. I thought of it as the UN-Civil War, but that was long ago; it now being 1885.

Whenever we were on the trail, Joe always carried his old single shot .22 rifle. He'd walk ahead until he got enough game for supper. He had already bagged a grouse, two squirrels and a jack rabbit for tonight's dinner. Joe was the cook of the outfit, except for biscuits and hot cakes – those were my specialty. He was planning to make stew with the day's bounty. We made camp, unloaded the mules and turned them out to forage. I started the fire and was gathering more firewood in the fading light, when a soft voice came out of the shadows.

I recognized the voice as my hand was halfway to my Army Colt .44 – it was my good friend, Black Cloud, who had the habit of always showing up at mealtime.

"How, Roy. I brought supper." He handed me a stick of firewood in the dark.

But, it wasn't a stick of wood! I had a rattle-snake squirming in my hand! I yelled and dropped it.

"Not afraid of a little snake, are you, Roy?"

"No! No! I just didn't know where the head was."

"I left it back by that big black rock where I found him," he said.

It gave Black Cloud great pleasure to get the best of me. Someday, just once, I'd like to put one over on him. "Come on in. You're welcome to the fire, but I don't know why." *It was the beginning of a most unusual night.*

That old Indian skinned the snake and handed it to Engine Joe for the pot. He also gave Joe some mushrooms, a wild onion and a squirrel from his pack.

Now, I don't know if you are aware of this or not, but when you're making stew you never, I mean *never* put in the left front leg of the rabbit. It's called the *humorous bone* and for good reason. A lot of people carry a rabbit's foot for good luck and you may have noticed that it's always the left front. You're about to find out why.

Well, I guess Joe got confused, with all the different types of game and all, because he chucked in the funny bone, too.

It was going to be an hour or more before the stew was done, so Black Cloud decided to make some biscuits using my secret recipe – a formula he had swindled me out of a few months ago when he saved my bacon. But that's a whole different story.

I asked the old Indian what he was doing on this bend of the trail and he told me he was trying to make a little money tracking four desperadoes who had held up a bank over in Grants Pass. The bandits killed a teller, a customer and a deputy, who just happened to be the sheriff's nephew. Sheriff Ketchem had been out-of-town fishing and he discovered the crime when he got back. He was furious and got up a posse and took off after them murdering coyotes.

"I chanced to come across the posse a couple days later and they hired me at a dollar a day to see if I could cut the trail of those killers. Well, we kept at it for three days and never did find hide nor hair of 'em. Now, there's a bounty of two hundred dollars a head, dead or alive and I think the sheriff would prefer 'em dead."

"That was a week ago, now I'm heading for Gold Beach to see Dancing Flower. I bought her a little gift with the money I made," said Black Cloud.

* * *

I heard the mules grazing just beyond the fire light and then a booming voice came out of the darkness. Drop your @#$%&* gun belts and nobody move; raise your @#$%^&* hands! Well, it looked like we'd been had – they had the drop on us. I raised my hands and said, "What do you want us to do, not move or drop our gun belts?"

"Don't get smart @#$%^&* old man, or we'll drop you in your tracks. Just ease off your @#$%^&* belt, nice and slow," the big voice said.

The voice sounded vaguely familiar and the foul lingo I knew for sure. It sounded like Bully Billy Boggs, but he was supposed to be dead! Boggs had been killed some six or seven years ago in an outhouse accident down on the Bogus River. Seems a tow line from a side-wheeler, the Rogue River Queen, got tangled around his outhouse and he was pulled all the way to Gold Beach before they noticed it. I'll bet he was flushed with excitement.

The sheriff said he must've been trying to get a free tow into Gold Beach and investigated the case no further. Bully Billy Boggs had bullied, humiliated, and terrorized his neighbors for fifteen years. Not one tear was shed in his behalf, but there sure were a lot of smiles as the news spread.

With our weapons on the ground, four shadows came into the firelight. Two of them were quite large.

"I recognize you," I said. "You're the Boggs boys, Billy Jr. and Brutus."

"And I recognize you, too, @#$%^&* old man. Now, just shut-up and tell us what the @#$%^&* you are doing here," said Brutus.

"Do you want me to shut up or tell you what we're doing here?"

I should have seen it coming. He caught me alongside the head with the barrel of his pistol. I had the feeling I was falling into the fire, but then strong arms pulled me aside at the last moment. It got dark and quiet.

I don't know how long I was out, but when I woke up, I tried to rub my aching head and found my hands were tied together. Then it all came back to me. Those Boggs boys were even meaner than their father had been and that was something.

They had two other bandits with them and all four of those miserable varmints were sitting around the fire with tin plates loaded with Engine Joe's stew. I watched quietly as they had seconds . . . then thirds . . . then fourths. Soon they were scraping the bottom of the pot. They seemed to get a little more cheerful with each plate of stew. By the time they were licking their plates, they were down right happy.

Then one of them pulled an old Wanted Poster out of his shirt pocket and showed it around. When Junior saw the likeness on the poster, he hooted with laughter until tears came to his eyes. He passed it on to the next fellow, who started laughing even before he saw the picture and when he did, he rolled on the ground holding his stomach and howling. Then Brutus grabbed the flyer and as soon as his eyes focused on it he doubled up with laughter. Then the scoundrel that started the poster going around said, "What's so funny." He picked up the fallen poster and when he looked at it, he also exploded with laughter, trying desperately to catch his breath. All four of the outlaws lay on the ground rolling back and forth, overcome with laughter and hooting and hollering. I'd never seen such a sight, well maybe once when I told a joke at the Green Lantern.

I looked across the fire at Joe – he was trussed up like a hog for slaughter and I could see him straining at his bonds. I made a little whistle and he looked over at me. I shook my head "NO!" he knew then I had a plan.

I asked Jr. if he would show me the poster. He couldn't stop laughing, but he held it up and giggled all the harder. I saw by the name on the Wanted Poster that one of the other fellows who had joined us for dinner was named Rex Bigalow.

"Hey Rex, if you got any more funny posters, I'd like to see 'em," I said.

"Sure, sure, I got lots." He laughed and pulled out a handful of crumpled papers and threw them at me.

I told him I didn't seem to be able to pick 'em up.

He looked over with his tear-filled eyes, still shaking with laughter. "Of course you can't – your hands are tied up."

He immediately convulsed into another spasm of laughter, as if it was the funniest thing he'd ever said. Then he stretched out on the ground, pulled his knife and with one careless swipe he cut my bonds.

I picked up the Wanted Posters, looked at one, started to laugh and passed it on. Soon I had all the posters going around the circle. Never in my life had

I seen such uncontrolled hoot'n an' holler'n. They were so weak from laughing, they couldn't even stand up.

I cut the rope from my ankles and crawled over to Engine Joe and cut him loose. He rubbed his wrists and ankles before he tried to stand, but when he did, he picked up two of the outlaws by the neck and banged their heads together with a terrible crack. The other two were still on the ground laughing so hard the tears just rolled down their faces and when they saw Joe pop their friends' noggins together, they thought it was the most hilarious thing they had ever seen. Even though Brutus was still laughing, he went for his six-shooter! I reached for my Colt! . . . But, of course, it wasn't there. I knew I was going to come in second and that was a one-way ticket to Boot Hill. I had started forward to kick the gun out of his hand, when a shot exploded out of the darkness. The revolver flew out of Bogg's bloody hand as Black Cloud stepped into the circle of light, my Army Colt, smok ing in his hand.

"This what you're looking for Roy?" The old Indian said quietly, a smile on his weathered face.

Darned if he didn't do it again – he saved my bacon. I'll never catch up with him at this rate. I didn't even wait for him to ask, because I already knew what he wanted. "All right, Black Cloud, you can have my Army Colt!"

Joe had the last Jasper on the ground and was hog-tying him for the night. In a few minutes he had 'em all in their *night clothes*, as he called it.

Well, to make a short story long, we took those four desperadoes all the way to Grants Pass, where they had a date with Sheriff Will Ketchem and a necktie party. The sheriff was sure happy to see us and said he was in our debt. He even offered to put us up in the hotel till the hanging. I thanked him, but said we had customers waiting on us and had to be getting along. We split the reward four ways, with a share going to the widow of the bank customer.

When I saw Sheriff Will about six months later, he said, "You know those hombres you brought in a few months back? Well, it was the strangest thing. They confessed to eleven stage holdups, four bank robberies and two train stickups. Laughing all the time like it was a big joke. I wired out all their aliases and there were more Wanted Posters on those desperadoes than you could shake a snake at. You and your partners got a passel of money coming. Let's head for the bank and get you paid off. You know, they laughed all the way through their trial. They even laughed while they were climbing the steps to the gallows. They all asked for stew for their last meal. Can you beat that? Very strange, very strange."

It sure was a big surprise – two thousand, four hundred dollars in reward money, split three ways. Why, that was almost enough to consider bounty hunting for a living, (but not for over one minute). Boy! Wouldn't Engine Joe and Black Cloud be surprised? Ya Hoo!

Now, about that stew. Joe thought it was the wild onion; Black Cloud thought it was the mushrooms; I thought it was the funny bone – anyway, it certainly was humorous.

THE END

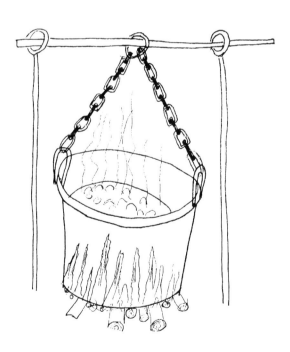

TALE TEN
HEAVENLY
HOTCAKES

I'm not one to brag, but when something is good, I mean really good and you want to share it, you have to tell how good it is. Well, I'd been making hotcakes on the trail for over thirty years and I finally stumbled on a recipe that made 'em so light and fluffy that they started to float right out of the pan. That's right – as soon as I flipped 'em, they started off for the heavens. There's always a drawback to every discovery and the drawback here was I could only cook one at a time. I didn't weigh enough to hold more than one down! To be perfectly truthful, the recipe, or at least half of it, came from Ma down at the Porthole Eatery in Gold Beach, Oregon. She's a mighty fine cook and a very independent lady.

As usual, I'm getting ahead of myself; so let me tell it like it happened:

Engine Joe and I were hauling supplies and a

little mail up the Rogue River in Oregon Territory. There was a group of miners that had struck it rich up past Big Bend and they needed food and equipment badly.

It was our first morning on the trail with eight heavily loaded mules and I was up early to fix breakfast. The sun was just about to break over the jagged hills that corralled the Rogue River on its way to the sea.

The cooking fire felt good against the morning chill. That's when I made the great discovery. I could hardly contain myself. I yelled at Joe to shake off them blankets and get over here and have some of the lightest hotcakes in the world. "No kidding, I have to hold em down!"

Sleepy-eyed Joe said, "I've always had a hard time keeping your hotcakes down, Roy."

"No! No! I mean these are *really* hard to keep down," I told him.

"And what I'm telling you, Roy, is that they're *really* hard to keep down. You make the best biscuits and oatmeal mush I ever ate, but your hotcakes are grim."

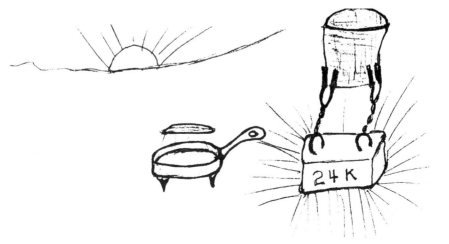

"O.K., just watch this," I said. I flipped another hotcake and when it started to rise from the skillet, I just let it go. That hotcake went straight up in the still air of the morning, reflecting the rising sun. As the griddle cake rose to about a hundred feet, I drew my Army Colt .44 and fired. With a puff, the hotcake deflated, did a few loops and swoops and then fell back to earth, much like a feather.

"Well, I'll be," Joe exclaimed, now fully awake. "Do that again."

We had so much fun shooting hotcakes that we ran out of batter, so I mixed up a double batch and we sat down to eat.

Now, let me tell you more about Joe. Like I said before, he was called *Engine* because he was as strong as the steam engine on the Rogue River Queen and he could work all day *balls out*, which means at full throttle. (The governor on a steam engine used the centrifugal force of spinning balls to keep it from running away. When they were spinning fast, the balls were as far out as they could go and that's where the expression *balls out* comes from.) His real name was Joseph J. Washington; he was six foot six inches tall, weighed over three hundred pounds and was black as the Queen's stacks. He was a man to stay on the good side of and a man to fear in a fight. Now, to get back to my story:

Well, it seemed that Joe couldn't get enough of those Heavenly Hotcakes and he ate till I thought he'd burst. Then the strangest thing happened: he started to rise up in the air! He shouted for me to do something, so I bent a sapling over to where he could reach it. The sapling held for a minute, but then just snapped off! I whipped out my lariat and caught Joe around the ankle and then tied him to a large fir tree. He kept yelling, "Do something! Do something!"

He floated like a hot-air balloon tied to that tree by a rope. Why he'd be a big hit in the Fourth of July parade at Gold Beach. I thought I'd have some fun with him. "Do you want me to shoot ya, Joe?" (I had visions of him looping and swooping around in the air like a blown-out balloon.)

"No! No! Just get me down! . . . Darn your hide; quit fooling around and get me down!"

I hadn't seen Joe that riled-up in a coon's age. I thought about it for awhile and then said, "I've got an idea." He sure did look funny bobbing around in the wind at the end of a rope. I just couldn't resist. "This the first time you been strung up, big fella." Then I hooted and slapped my leg and doubled up with laughter. The roar of his Walker .44 wiped the grin off my face, but the recoil wrapped him halfway round the tree.

"Hold on, Joe, let me get some of the girls." The only way I could figure to keep him on the ground was to have him carry one of the mules. Well, one mule wouldn't do it, so he had to pick up two of 'em to keep him on the ground. If that wasn't a sight, him walking into the miner's camp carrying two mules loaded down with equipment. The miners all stood there with their mouths wide open, frozen in position. I had to go around shutting their mouths so they could start talking again. Joe set one of the mules down and it seemed like he was going to stay on the ground. Then he put the other mule down and found out he was back to normal, or as normal as he was normally, which wasn't normally that normal.

We unloaded all the animals and passed out the goods, but the miners still stood there dumb-founded. They weren't going to let us leave without an explanation. It was then I told my first lie, ever. I had to protect my new recipe, of course. I told them the mules were so heavily loaded that Joe had to carry them the last few feet into camp – actually it was more like twenty-two miles.

Those miners were still a little suspicious and didn't quite believe what they had seen, but it didn't stop them from having a *hootdown* celebration. Those miners would party at the pop of a cork *and* furnish the bottle it popped out of.

The subject of payment came up and they paid us off in gold. They had a great big box loaded with the shiny stuff that must've weighed twelve hundred pounds. I asked them if they weren't afraid some one would rob them of their hard-worked-for treasure. "Heck no," the lead miner replied. "It's so heavy no one can lift it."

I really hate to butt into a man's business, but these gents were asking for trouble. That much gold was like a magnet for every desperado in this neck of the woods. It could get them all killed and anybody else that happened to be around.

I outlined the dangers: "Did you ever hear of Yellow Dog, Bully Boggs, Larry Loud, the Vermillions, or Marvin Meanest? How about the Waymen Brothers? Any one of them would slit your throat, for the fun of it. They're the worst bunch of killers that ever slapped leather. They'll dry gulch yah', back shoot yah', torture yah', and burn yah' alive, and that's not even the bad stuff they do to yah'."

I also offered to help: "Tell yah' what we'll do. Joe and I will transport your gold to the Bank of Oregon in Grants Pass and deposit it for a fee of only five percent. The banker is a friend of my father's from Missouri and he can be trusted. His name is Irwin B. Upright. He is as honest as they come."

After talking it over, they decided to let us take the gold and deposit it in the bank for the agreed upon charge; as long as we guaranteed its safe arrival. We shook hands on it and that was all that was needed to seal the agreement. The only other thing they wanted was to melt the gold down into one big nugget to make it real hard for any bandit to walk away with it.

Well, it took about two days for them galoots to get all that gold melted down and when they were done, they had a block of gold just about one foot square. At my request they stuck a couple mule shoes in the top of the gold block just as it hardened up. Someone popped a cork and they had another hootdown to celebrate the making of the big nugget.

Early the next morning, I was up at the crack of dawn mixing up a batch of my Heavenly Hotcakes.

The miners were still sleeping off the previous night's cork-pop'n and only a couple of 'em stirred when I called Engine Joe for a breakfast of lighter than air fare.

We took a couple of feed bags and tied them with short ropes to the mule shoes stuck in the gold and, as I turned the hotcakes, Joe slipped them into the bags one at a time. As unbelievable as it seems, it only took six hotcakes on each side to *float the gold* – but then they were big hotcakes. We tethered the gold to a tree while we continued our preparations to get underway.

I yelled *R. O. P. E. and* Ruby, Opal, Pearl and Emerald came a'running. They lined up in order, eager to be on the trail again. Then I yelled *R. O. P. E. Two* and Rose, Olga, Patti and Evelyn came walking slowly out of the woods. They were not so eager to be second team, so I gave 'em all a little piece of hotcake to lighten their spirits. Then we hit the trail for Grants Pass.

Engine Joe picked up the big nugget – actually he was holding it down – and headed up the trail with long, buoyant steps. A groggy, sleepy-eyed miner looked up from his bedroll, saw Joe floating up the trail carrying the big block of gold and then lay back down. He popped up a second later with a look of disbelief on his face, shook his head and fell back to sleep.

Now that much gold in one place is going to be like a carcass on the desert attracting buzzards. Gold news travels fast amongst bad people. I didn't like the idea of Engine Joe carrying that gold without his gun-hand free, because it made him an easy target. We tied the gold securely above Rose, who was in the middle of the pack string and was the most sure-footed of the pack mules.

*   *   *

It was a surprise, but it wasn't totally unexpected, when a couple of shots rang out and a big voice boomed out right after them.

"Stick-Em-Up or I'll drop you where you stand!"

I recognized the voice – there was only one voice that loud and cruel - Larry Loud. He had the loudest voice in the world. It hurt your ears even when he whispered. He was not only loud, he was mean to boot – I mean really mean.

I saw him shoot a man back a few years ago in Gold Beach just for taking the last piece of blackberry pie at the Port Hole Restaurant. He was out-of-town before the sheriff knew what happened. The posse tried to cut his trail, but he disappeared without a trace. This was the first I'd heard of him since then.

"Throw down your shootin' irons and be quick about it, or be dead!" The booming voice said.

I still couldn't see him, what with all the brush along the trail, but I bet he could see me. I unbuckled my gun belt and let it slip to the ground.

"I said, 'drop it,' fool!"

Apparently, he *couldn't* see me, because he was

talking at Joe. I scooped up my gun belt and headed back down the trail as quietly as I could. My plan was to circle around and get the drop on him from behind.

"Where's the gold, big fella. Don't give me any trouble and you'll live to see another sunrise."

I heard Engine Joe say back at him, "It's on Rose, the fifth mule back. I'll call her up here."

I'll bet Joe has a plan.

Joe gave a whistle to Rose. "Rose! C'mon gal."

Rose moved past the other mules on the side of the trail and made quite a bit of noise crashing through the brush. I used the noise to cover me as I moved into position. Then I saw him. It *was* Larry Loud and he had a sawed-off shotgun aimed at Joe's middle. *Never go up against a shotgun with a pistol – I better just wait and see what happens.*

When Larry saw the huge gold nugget floating above the mule, he blinked and shook his head. "What the devil? If you're trying to pull something on me, I'll shoot you deader than graveyard dead." He slipped the shotgun under his arm and started to untie the buoyant nugget. He grinned when it came loose and he could hold it in his hands. "Well, I'll be!" He exclaimed as he carried the gold back towards Joe, past the lead mule.

As soon as he was clear of Rose and Joe, I took my shot, right through one of the feed bags. It started to whip around as one of the pancakes started its whoopee-dupe and rapped the rope around the robber's neck. Joe pulled out his belly-gun and shot the other bag, which did the same thing only in the other direction. As the gold lost its flotation ability, it crashed to the ground pulling Larry Loud with it. I heard both of his ankles break as he fell. *Now* he wasn't smiling. The shotgun discharged as it hit the ground, blowing the heel off his right boot. He howled a terrible howl that shook the pine needles from the trees miles away.

His troubles were just beginning. We hog-tied and then blindfolded him, and strapped him to one of the mules for his trip to Grants Pass and Sheriff Ketchem's jail. There was a reward for his capture Dead or Alive and we planned to collect it, as well as the commission for transporting the gold. Boy, were we having fun! And making money, too!

Then I remembered that the last time he had been captured, he started to yell so loud that Sheriff Pokey Smith dropped his six-guns so he could but his fingers in his ears. Larry got the drop on him and escaped. I told Joe we had better gag this varmint or he might do the same thing to us.

There was still some daylight left, so after building a fire and cooking some replacement hotcakes to float the gold we were on the trail again.

*   *   *

The shadows were growing long and the first cool breeze of the evening told me it was time to make camp. Joe had bagged a couple of grouse as he led the pack train out of the deep Rogue River canyon and I was so hungry I could already taste'm. I yelled to Joe to stop at the next likely looking camping spot and he said he already had one in mind just a little ways ahead by a small creek. I smelled smoke just about then and the undeniable odor of bacon frying.

We halted the mule train and both Joe and I walked ahead cautiously with our shooting irons at the ready. As we entered the little clearing, we saw a woman bending over a campfire stirring something in a frying pan. We were close enough to hear the bacon sizzle. She had one of those sunbonnets on and the brim nearly covered her face. We both holstered our six-guns. I said, "Hello the fire." But she didn't seem startled; she just waved us in and kept cooking. Something just didn't seem right, but I thought *I'm just a little nervous because of the gold and the events of the day.*

As I stood across the fire from her, she looked up at me. Now, I've seen some ugly women in my day, but this one would have looked better if she'd been stuck by lightning. She spoke, "Like to have some fun, old man?" Her ugly face cracked in two with a big grin.

We'd been had! It was Little Meaney, so Big Meaney could not be far away. A voice came out of the shadows, "Throw down your things . . . and leather stuff – I've got the fall on you."

"No! No! Darn it! I've got the drop on you. How many times do I have to tell ya? It's the *drop* not *fall.*" Little Meaney shouted to Big Meaney. He began taking off his disguise. Then he looked at us standing with our hands raised.

"Do you mind?" he said, with a toss of his head, as he started to slip the dress off.

Joe and I both turned around with our hands still raised. We both realized we been had again and turned back to see Little Meaney doubled-up with laughter.

It didn't take much to figure out who was the brains in this outfit. Joe and I both dropped our gun belts – this was getting to be a bad habit.

We had heard stories about these two robbers for years and all the jobs they had pulled and how they'd messed 'em up. One time, over by Grants Pass, they were going to hold-up the stagecoach in the wintertime. The stage was an hour late on a really cold, windy day. As the coach got to the top of the pass (it was going quite slow after the long steep grade), the driver saw the two desperadoes with their guns drawn standing in the middle of the road. The driver stopped the horses just in time and waited for the robbers to say something. They just stood there and then he realized they were frozen stiff and had icicles hanging off their beards. The driver and the man riding shotgun just picked 'em up and moved 'em to the side of the road. As the stagecoach drove out of sight, they looked back to see 'em still standing there with their pistols drawn. I'll bet they never lived that one down. Then there was the time over by Bandon when . . . well that's a whole different story. I better get back to my hotcake tale.

Little Meany, who was only about five feet tall,

yelled at his big brother, who was over six feet, to pick up the gun belts and be quick about it.

He looked at us and said, "Now, where's that gold I been hearing about?"

"It's back on one of the mules; I'll go get it."

Little Meany meant business. "No you don't – you're trying to pull a fast one on us. I'll get it myself – my mom didn't raise no fools."

"You're probably an orphan then," I said under my breath.

"What's that?" Are you getting smart with me? What did you say?" The little man was getting more angry.

"I said it's not 'ore then." It's been melted into one big glob. Let me call the mule that's carrying it and she'll bring it right to you. O.K.?"

"All right, but no tricks." Little Meany stood waiting, fidgeting with his pistol.

I called to Rose and she came walking up the trail and stopped right in front of me and Joe – just as nice as you please. The big golden nugget was floating above her, bobbing in the evening breeze.

"Is this some kinda a joke? Are you trying to pull something on me?" Little Meany walked over to the mule, holstered his six-gun and pulled out his pocketknife. He carved a little sliver of gold off the corner of the glob. He looked it over real careful and then put it in his mouth and bit it with his teeth. "It's really gold. What's going on here?" He stood on his tiptoes and reached up into the feed bag and started to pull out one of the hotcakes.

"I wouldn't do that if I were you," I said.

He looked at me defiantly. "You're not me, old man."

As soon as that hotcake cleared the edge of the bag, it started to rise, taking the little fellow with it. He was so startled that he hung on and soon he was too high up to let go.

"Help! Help! Save me!" he screamed.

"I'd like to help, but I'm just an old man," I yelled up to him, as he kept going higher and higher.

Big Meany was becoming alarmed – it must've been like a man in a canoe watching his paddle floating down stream.

"What did you do to my brother?" He began to sob and pointed his old cap-n-ball revolver at us. "Bring him back or I'll shoot ya."

"We can't bring him back, but you can join him if'n ya want too."

"O. K., but no silly business."

"Come over here to this feedbag and take out one of these hotcakes and don't let go." I untied the rope holding the gold to old Rose and it settled to the ground. Joe reached up into the bag and handed Big Meany one of those wonderful, buoyant discs. Then he took Big Meany's revolver away and put a hotcake in his other hand. With a frightened look on his face, Big Meany's feet left the ground and he started to rise up in the air.

"What should I do? What should I do?" He was in somewhat of a panic.

"Just hold on; don't let go and soon you'll be

with your brother."

I almost felt sorry for the bumbling big guy as he floated higher and higher towards his brother, who was now a speck in the sky.

*   *   *

The rest of our journey was uneventful. We arrived in Grants Pass a few days later and turned Larry Loud over to Sheriff Ketchem and collected our bounty. Then it was on to the bank to deposit the huge gold nugget. We had to wait till dark to leave the gold at the bank so no one would see how we transported it. They never did figure it out and we never told 'em.

In case you're wondering about what happened to the Meany brothers, we heard rumors of an outlaw gang in Australia that pulled so many bonehead stunts that it kept the local papers busy writing about them. There was a little guy and a big guy that led them.

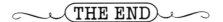

THE END

Oh, by the way, if you don't believe Roy about the hotcakes, take a look at the power lines that cross the Rogue River just upstream of Governor Patterson Bridge. You see those big orange balls that keep the wires up? You guessed it; they're filled with some of Roy's old hotcakes. How else could something so small float those big wires?   Lewis Cannon

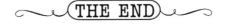

THE END

TALE ELEVEN
THE MAGIC SAW

Some remember it as the day the Devil came to the Rogue River Valley – to others it was just an unusually hot day, even for mid-August. There was something queer about the stranger with the bright, red suspenders and easy ways. A pleasant enough character, but then peddlers usually are. He arrived in a spiffy wagon drawn by a matched pair of black horses that were so much alike they looked as if they were tapped out of the same mold.

There was something strange about his magnificent horses. They didn't seem to have any spirit and they had a look of terror in their eyes. Children didn't try to be friendly with these brooding, silent beasts, who acted as if they were in chains and not in harness.

A massive black dog guarded the wagon when the master was absent – he was as black as the soot in a stovepipe and as shy to the sunlight. He would lunge at anyone foolish enough to come too near, show his ample teeth, and then retreat back into the shadows. The brute was mute, but his heavy chains gave him voice.

The wagon was full of tempting goods meant to raise the desire of any mortal, no matter what their secret passion. There were beautiful dolls with golden hair to cause longing in proper little girls and sling-shots and jackknives for boisterous boys. For the ladies, bolts of colorful cloth, too bright for church, but just right to say *look at me!* For men, the peddler had sharp razors with black leather strops and sweet-smelling water. There were nickel-plated revolvers that came in velvet cases and pocket watches with pictures engraved on the back. Guarantees were implied with winks and smiles and hardy laughs.

* * *

A lot of the men in town gathered at the old Port Hole Pub and Eatery to talk about politics and tell tall tales. This was usually during the rainy season, which only lasts from October first to September thirtieth on the South Coast.

I was one of the favorite storytellers, but mostly I sat back and listened. But when I did start one of my own, everyone got quiet. No one wanted to miss a single word. Even the pretty waitress, Rose Marie, stopped serving and stood close by to listen to the captivating stories.

There were tales of wild animals, of extreme

weather, of large fish, of unusual people, of strange places and mysterious happenings. They were filled with daring deeds, adventure and humor, all told with compassion. No hero went unrewarded; no bully unpunished; justice was always served. There was a lesson to be learned, a moral to be remembered and a warning to those wise enough to heed it. Above all, they were just plain fun.

A clatter of hooves outside announced the arrival of a wagon and the stomping of boots on the boardwalk indicated the driver was coming into the Port Hole. It was the traveling salesman, the peddler, the one with the fancy wagon and sinister horses. He strode into the saloon boldly, nodding greetings and smiling at everyone as if he had lived there all his life.

He was a handsome looking gentleman. His age was really hard to tell, not young, but then not really old either. His clothes were well made and stylish, but just a little too colorful for these parts. He reminded people of a politician or a lawyer – a little too slick and not to be trusted with anything of value such as a vote or the deed to a property.

The stranger found a vacant table in the rear and called for the waitress with the wave of his hand. I had just started telling an engrossing tale and Rose Marie was totally lost in the story. I saw what was about to happen, so I stopped in mid-sentence, got to my feet, and said, "I better check on my mule string." Amid the moans and groans of my listeners, I excused myself and headed for the door. I called back over my shoulder that I would be back in two shakes of a lamb's tail.

When I returned to the restaurant, everyone had been served and the general clatter of dishes and conversation filled the air. I tried to slip quietly into my favorite booth, but one of the other customers spotted me and asked for me to continue the story. I began a new tale and soon had the whole room on pins and needles. I had them laughing and crying, angry and sad and then at the end, they hooted and laughed till the tears ran down their faces.

When I left that afternoon, the smiling stranger slapped me on the back and said he'd sell his soul to be able to tell a tale like that. I always look a man in the eye when I speak to him, but when I looked into the peddler's eyes I was afraid of what I saw and looked away quickly. The face was smiling, but the eyes were deadly serious. They were like two black pools that you could drown in.

That night, on the trail up river, I had a terrible nightmare that was too horrible to tell. I couldn't sleep, so I built up the fire and put on some biscuits for breakfast. My four mules were grazing near the fire, which cast a flickering, yellow light against the scrub pine trees. I lay back against one of the packs and went over the days events in my mind . . . zzzzz.

A twig snapped . . . ! My hand hovered over my Army Colt revolver . . . . A voice boomed out of the darkness . . . "Hello the fire!"

"Who's there," I called out.

"Why it's only me, the old peddler man." He emerged from the shadows.

I kept my hand on my gun and invited the phantom to share the fire and my coffee. Sure enough, it *was* the traveling salesmen. But I wondered how a stranger to these here parts could find his way up a dangerous river canyon at night. It was very puzzling.

We talked for awhile, sipping our coffee, and then the peddler got to the point. He asked me to come with him on his wagon. We would travel the world selling his goods and all I would have to do is tell stories to gain the trust of his potential customers. For this I would be paid ONE HUNDRED DOLLARS A DAY, IN GOLD!

I was stunned at the offer – there must be more to it than that. An offer that was too good to be true usually wasn't. As I was contemplating his generous proposal, the colorful stranger spoke again.

"All you have to do is sign this contract and the money is yours, Mister McCoy."

Now, two things bothered me: I hated contracts and how in the *devil* did this Jasper know my last name? There weren't but three or four people in the whole Rogue River Valley that knew my *real* last name and none of them had been in town today.

"Let me look over that contract and I'll let you know in the morning."

The peddler lost his smile and put the offered pen back in his pocket. He was a little red under the collar but shook it off, then smiled, becoming once again a congenial fellow.

I examined the contract carefully, noticing the

fine vellum it was written on and the excellent pen-manship – although some of the words were quite archaic.

Everything seemed straight-forward, until I noticed that the cursive lines of the text were made up of miniature words no thicker than the line itself. Curious, I reached into my pack and brought out a magnifying glass in order to read the tiny print. It said something about "trading your soul for . . . ." Suddenly, the stranger ripped the document out of my hand and quickly rolled it up, his face red with fury. He was shaking with rage and his voice trembled with barely controlled anger as he said, "Think you're smart, do you? I'll get you yet! *No one* gets the best of me."

There was a gust of wind, the fire flared and the angry man disappeared into the night like smoke from a flame. Fumes from the fire caused my eyes to water and I wasn't quite sure what I had just seen, all I knew was that the peddler was gone.

The next morning, I backtracked a little ways and although I was one of the best trackers in the valley, I couldn't find a trace of the strange peddler. Things were sure getting strange.

*   *   *

Before I tell the next part of this tale, I need to tell you that *Illinois River McCoy* was the name of my younger brother's son, but most people called him *Mac.* He was named after the river he was born near some twenty years ago. Yellow Dog, a renegade Indian, had killed my brother Ringo some fifteen years before in an ambush.

I tracked Yellow Dog for over a year without success. It was as if he had disappeared off the face of the earth. I thought I had him once, but it was his twin brother, Blue Dog, a courageous Indian who was also hunting his brother. He intended to bring him to justice for the horrible deeds he had done to his tribe. They tracked him together for a few months without success and then parted company the best of friends.

That was in the past now and one best get on with his life by keeping busy and being useful.

From that time on, I had looked after Mac and his mother Mavis. I spent the Fourth of July and my birthday every year at their ranch.

*   *   *

Mac was coming back to the cabin for his noon meal, when a stranger entered the clearing with a wagon pulled by a pair of beautiful black horses. The wagon was loaded with all kinds of goods and supplies. Mac wondered what the stranger was doing in these parts, because his Uncle Roy was the only person whoever came to this neck of the woods.

The peddler gave a big hello and a smile to match – he seemed a nice enough fellow. Just then Mac's mother, Mavis, came out on the porch to see what all the commotion was about. She raised her hand above her eyes to better see the handsome stranger and said *Oh my!* to herself.

The tall, dapper man whipped off his hat and bowed deeply. "Good day beautiful lady; you're the prettiest thing I've seen in a month of Sundays. I'm Mr. Lived and I carry with me all you desire."

Mavis blushed. "Wipe your feet and leave the rest of the blarney outside. You're welcome to come in for dinner."

When the peddler entered the cabin, he was carrying a small wrapped packet. He handed it to Mrs. McCoy. "Take this with my compliments, Madam, as a gift with no obligations."

She was so flustered by the handsome man that she accepted the present, something she would normally never do – not from a complete stranger. Mavis unwrapped the small package and found a sewing kit, complete with scissors, pin cushion and a nifty little needle threader. She thanked the man and started to serve dinner.

The dapper salesman was quite witty and entertained them with stories of his adventures on the road all through the meal.

Mac told him that they only did business with his Uncle Roy and that he was just wastin' his time here. Mac didn't like the way Mr. Lived was fawning over his mother and wished he would leave.

The handsome stranger asked Mac to come outside because there was something he wanted to show him, a special tool from the old country. The peddler reached into his wagon and pulled out something long that was wrapped in heavy canvas.

Unwrapping the canvas, Mac saw that it was a cross cut saw with teeth as shiny as diamonds. The handles were crafted of a fine dark wood and carved with scenes of trees, stags, mountains and streams. It was the most elegant tool Mac had ever seen, better than even the walnut stock on his rifle, *but then pretty doesn't get the job done, sweat does.* Even the curved guard for the teeth had fancy carvings on it – it was truly a thing of beauty.

Mac was thinking he really needed a new cross-cut. His old one had been filed to the nubs with years of use. The price must be out of this world. His thoughts were interrupted by the peddler, as if he was reading his mind.

"Don't say a thing until you try it. I know you'll be amazed." The peddler smiled. "I'll make you an offer you can't refuse."

Now, the most important thing in the whole world to Mac was his sweetheart, Rose Marie. They were planning to get married as soon as they could save enough money. She was working as a waitress down at the Port Hole and saving all she could. Rose was the town beauty. All the local fellows hung around the café trying to make time with her, but she only had eyes for Illinois "Mac" McCoy.

Mac was putting in long days cutting cedar trees

and splitting fence posts for the ranchers in the valley. He was a real hard worker and back then that was the best compliment you could pay a man, right after you said he was honest. With a little luck they would soon have enough money to buy the old Johnson place, with some left over for a nice wedding.

Mac picked out a log to try the saw on and started his cut. He thought the saw might bite in a little on the first stroke, but it was so smooth he couldn't believe it! The next stroke was effortless and yet the saw bit deep in the wood. It almost felt as if someone was pulling on the back stroke. In a flash, he was through the log. On the next cut, he speeded up a little and the saw hummed through the cut. At normal working speed, it sounded like one of those saws down at the fairground that the fiddlers play – it had a wailing, haunting sound.

Before Mac realized it, the entire log was cut up and he wasn't even sweating. Boy! He had to have this saw! With the new crosscut he could cut enough wood to pay for the saw and save sufficient money to get married by Thanksgiving. They wouldn't have to wait till Christmas.

The peddler watching him closely and when Mac smiled, the man told him the price: thirteen dollars in GOLD! That was a lot of money for a crosscut saw, but this was no ordinary saw.

"I want it, but I don't have thirteen dollars in gold," Mac said.

"Don't worry about it young man. I'll collect the

next time I come through. Just sign this here little ol' paper that sez you owe it to me and it's a deal."

"I don't know about that. I never signed no paper before. My Uncle Roy always takes care of that kinda legal stuff."

"Well, you're in luck, son. I'm a very good friend of your Uncle Roy. Why we spent last night together on the trail west of here," Mr. Lived said. "And he knows how *honest* I am. Besides, I'm the one trusting *you* to pay for the saw.

Mac was looking over the saw one last time, when he pricked his finger on the extremely sharp teeth and a drop of blood fell on the contract! Without a lost motion, the traveling gent produced a quill from nowhere, dipped it in the blood and had Mac sign his name before he realized what had happened.

"Now son, I'll be back through these parts along about October third and we'll settle up then."

While the stranger waited for the *ink* to dry before he rolled the document, Mac glanced at the contract and noticed his name was printed near the line by his signature, *Illinois River McCoy. How in thunder did this Jasper know his full name? Something queer was happening. Maybe Uncle Roy told him. That is if they really did camp together last night. Hmmmm?*

*   *   *

The time flew by quickly and summer was soon a pleasant memory. It was the time of year that makes a person reflective – some happy, some sad, some a little of both. It was my birthday. I would be fifty-five years old on October third. I was headed for Mavis and Mac's place near the juncture of the Rogue and Illinois Rivers, about twenty-six miles from the Pacific Ocean. It didn't seem like I had been rattling around these parts for more than twenty years, but I looked in a mirror a couple of years ago and figured I was just getting old on the outside.

Mavis made some of the best Apple Pie in the whole of Curry County and for my birthday every year she made me pie instead of cake. It was well worth waiting a year for. When I pulled my mule train into the clearing at their ranch, I saw a pair of horses, black as Satan's whip, already there. My nephew was on the porch, face-to-face with the mysterious peddler.

Mac was shouting at him, while Mavis held a handkerchief to her pretty face, sobbing uncontrollably. The peddler was holding up a large paper and shaking it in Mac's face. I loosened the loop on the hammer of my Colt .44 and strode towards the cabin. I felt the anger rising in my throat. *When anyone picked on kith or kin, I was cocked and primed for trouble.*

I quickly mounted the stops. "What's going on here?"

Everyone started talking at once and with such passion that I couldn't make head or tails out of what they were saying.

"Hold your horses! Hold your horses!" I said. "One at a time, now. Com'on Mac, let's take a walk."

I looked at the sharpie. "You stay here, mister," I said in a barely-controlled voice.

"I'm so glad you're here, Roy," said Mavis. She dried her tears and went inside to finish making dinner. *Women always have to work, whether during triumph or tragedy.*

As I strolled with my nephew, he told me about the wonderful saw he had bought from the deceitful huckster and the contract he had signed because he didn't have thirteen dollars in gold to pay for it. He had more than enough money now, almost two hundred dollars, but the shyster wouldn't take it. He wanted the contract fulfilled as agreed upon. There was some fine print that the boy wasn't even aware of. It that said if he didn't pay the money back by October first, he would have to travel with the peddler for a period of five years as a wagon-driver or his mom would lose the ranch. Mac told him the traveling man didn't even show up till today, two days late.

"This isn't about you," I told Mac. "This is between me and that devil of a man. He tried to cheat me back in August and I caught him at it – now he's trying to get at me through you and your ma. You see, he knew this was my birthday and I would be here today. He had it all planned out, the slimy critter."

Mac was really worried because if he had to go with the peddler he couldn't get married to Rose Marie. Maybe she wouldn't wait and his whole life would be ruined.

"Now don't fret yourself, son, just leave every-thing to me. This is my fight." When we got back to the front porch, the fancy peddler was rocking back and forth in one of Mavis' porch chairs with a smug smile on his face, smoking his pipe.

"I guess I'm gonna have a new traveling companion with me, one way or another," he said, pointing his pipe stem directly at me.

"Show me that contract, sir," I said, ignoring his jibe. "Mac, you go in the cabin and stay there with your mother until I tell you to come out."

The huckster produced the contract and I walked off the porch to the south side of the cabin to study it. I unrolled it and tacked it to the wall, using the butt of my Colt .44. Then I pulled my magnifying glass out of my shirt pocket and proceeded to exam-ine the document. I looked it over from top to bottom but couldn't find a single thing out of the ordinary.

"If you want to do the job, you have to have the correct tool," the smug-looking peddler said. He pulled a large banjo-shaped package out of the wagon and unwrapped the largest magnifying glass I had ever seen. It must've been over three feet across and weighed sixty pounds. A glass that size took two people to manage it, so the stranger held it and I focused it.

"Now, you see that period at the very end of the agreement, the one just a little larger than the rest? Look at that; it's all there."

I adjusted the glass and the words popped into view.

Sure enough, it was all there, twelve paragraphs of the finest legalese, Latin lawyer, double-talk, airtight, sans loophole rhetoric of which any shyster would be proud. It was an ironclad agreement giving the ranch to the stranger. It was signed in blood and was legal in this world *or any other.*

"You come traveling with me, Roy and I'll forget about this contract. I want to enjoy your stories in a strange land where it's hotter than blazes." The evil one looked at me with a self-satisfied grin.

Then the sun broke through the clouds and I focused the beam of the magnifying glass to a fine point, right on the period being discussed. Instantly, the spot burst into flame! It was gone in a puff of smoke, leaving a small hole with blackened edges. The peddler dropped the glass and beat at the paper with his bare hand, but it was too late.

"Now, where was that fine print you wanted me to look at, sir?"

His smile disappeared and in its place appeared the most hideous face ever seen by man. His eyes turned bright red, like hot coals. Smoke started to pour out of his nostrils and red flames came from his mouth as he spoke. He shouted at the cabin and it burst into flames. "I'll teach you to mock me!"

I felt myself engulfed in flames. I could smell the biscuits burning. Biscuits burning? I awoke with a start. My boot was smoking and my foot felt like it was on fire! Black smoke rolled out of the Dutch oven. There wasn't any cabin on fire. I was waking up now and trying to shuck off my hot smoldering boot as fast as I could.

My heart was pounding in my chest and the sun was shining in my face. Then I realized it was only a dream. Thank goodness! It was still August and I was just starting a trip. What a relief.

A nightmare – I knew it was a nightmare – because I didn't get any Apple Pie. Well, maybe I should go a little out of the way and check on Mavis and Illinois, and possibly solve the pie problem, too.

At least I would have another tall tale to tell.

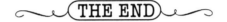

THE END

TALE
TWELVE
DISAPPEARING MULES

When I left Grants Pass early in the morning one day in late August, the sky was the color of a robin's egg and the smell of summer floated on the gentle breeze that played amongst the cedar branches. I vowed that nothing was going to spoil this glorious day. I could hear the rat-tat-tat of a woodpecker searching out his breakfast on an old hollow snag near the trail that meandered along the Rogue River. The sun was already warm on my back, as the two heavily loaded mules and I walked along the trail on our way to the new gold strike up at Shady Lady Mine.

It was a big strike and every would-be miner was heading out to make his fortune. The bad news was that every bad man, desperado, bandit and lawyer would also be heading for the new gold diggings to steal whatever they could.

I had decided to take only two of my mules because I was delivering mostly woman's stuff that I had picked up at the railroad station in town. It was a rush order all the way from Paris, France – whoop-de-do and la-de-DA!

Some "fancy ladies" had ordered dresses, perfume and a bunch of women's junk that they just *had* to buy with their newfound wealth. It wasn't totally foolish – they also had six cases of French wine listed on the bill-of-lading. The total cost was three hundred and thirty-three dollars, which was a lot of money in 1888.

It was a great day, but something was wrong. There was something in the air – it smelled like low tide! Low tide? How could it be the tide-flats? We were well over a hundred miles from the ocean beaches of the Oregon Coast. The smell kept getting stronger and stronger. It was definitely low tide or something like it or worse.

I looked up in the sky and saw buzzards circling high overhead. Maybe I was getting near the source of that rotten smell?

Then a voice shouted from the brush, "Hello Roy!"

It was a voice I recognized instantly – but what in tarnation was Black Cloud doing in this corner of the woods?

"Howdy, Black Cloud, what in . . . ?"

"You're wondering what in tarnation I'm doing in this corner of the woods," he interrupted. He stepped out from behind a bush. For some reason he always knew what I was thinking.

"I brought a few gifts to Dancing Flower after you gave me that reward money and I thought I'd spend a little time around the lodge, but in a few days, her talk-talk-talk was like a drum in my ear. I had to leave and when I did, she gave me a special charm to protect me. I guess it's working. Everybody seems to be keeping their distance."

"I can tell you this, old friend; that charm is doing its job. First of all it's got your nose so plugged up you can't smell anything and secondly, you stink so bad even a skunk would double blink and back away from you. And another thing, I'll bet she made you wear it to keep the other squaws away from you while you were out wandering around."

"You sure, Roy? I can't smell a thing."

"These watering eyes ain't lyin', Black Cloud. You'd better get rid of that bag around your neck before somebody replaces it with a noose!"

The old Indian removed the little leather pouch and twirled it around and around like a sling. Then he let it fly high in the air. I couldn't resist, I drew my Colt .44 and fired just as it reached its high point. I've done some impulsive things in my life and I've done some stupid things, but this had to be the worst of both.

When that chunk of lead hit that little poke, all hell broke loose. An explosion of green mist covered everything for a hundred feet in every direction. And the smell! I never smelled anything that bad in my whole life. Both my mules, Ruby and Opal, snorted and headed down the trail in a near panic with Black Cloud and me right behind 'em.

I heard a crashing noise off to the left and

darned if some buzzards didn't get a whiff of that green stuff and fell out of the sky, stone cold dead!

There was a small stream at the bottom of the next gully and I quickly hung my hardware on a tan oak branch and dove in head first, clothes and all.

I staggered out of the water after floundering around for a few minutes and darned if I didn't smell just as bad as before.

Evidently the water had started to clear up Black Cloud's nose. As he rose up out of the little pool, he exclaimed, "What's that smell? It's like old, wet moccasins on a hot summer day." Then he blew his nose and sniffed again. "Nope, it don't smell that good."

I found the mules a'ways down the path and tried to lead them back up the trail to the little creek, but they didn't want any part of it. They got real stubborn and wouldn't budge. I took a couple of bandanas, crushed some pungent myrtle leaves inside them, and then hung 'em over their noses. That did the trick and both mules followed me back to where Black Cloud was still in the pool trying to wash that horrible stink off. He helped me unload the mules and then I gently coaxed them into the water to hopefully scrub some of the stench off 'em.

I don't normally break into my customer's goods when I'm packing, but this was an emergency. I broke open one of the crates and took out two bars of that fancy French soap and tossed one to Black Cloud. I started washing myself, clothes and all. Boy, did that soap smell good and strong, but maybe a little too good.

I'll bet it took the better part of an hour to get that green stink scrubbed off us and then we started scrubbing the mules. We were just finishing up when I heard a twig snap!

A voice came out of the shadows – a kinda whispery voice. "What are you ladies doing on such a fine summer's day?"

Then there was an explosion of laughter, as a half dozen voices hooted and hollered. I instinctively went for my shooting iron, only to realize I was naked as a jaybird with my six-gun hanging on a branch some ten feet away. It was most em-bare-assing. Another round of laughter broke out, as I stood there with my hand grasping the air near my hip. A bunch of shady-looking characters began to emerge from the surrounding brush.

It seems the older I get, the more people get the drop on me. I decided then and there that I had better change my ways, and soon. If I lived through this, I'd never live it down.

As the mules and I clamored out of the pool, Black Cloud took the opportunity to slip quietly under the water and disappear downstream without a sound.

"Hey! What happened to that Indian who was here a second ago?" one of the desperadoes shouted. Everyone looked around, but no one saw hide nor hair of him – he had simply vanished.

The one with the wispy voice pulled his six-iron and threw five shots downstream in the general direction he thought Black Cloud might have gone. To everyone's surprise there was a yelp, a thud, and then silence. Deafening silence. Only the bubbling of the little creek could be heard.

"Do you want me to go take a look-see boss?" one of them asked the leader.

"No, an old, naked, unarmed Indian won't be giving us any trouble," the gunman whispered, "besides we got these here mule packs to check out."

I knew by the ugly scar circling the ringleader's neck he must be Whispering Will, the notorious bank robber and all-around bad guy. He had been caught once and hung for cattle rustling, but he was cut down after the posse rode off. Unfortunately, he survived and developed a reputation that he couldn't be killed. Whispering Will Willard had been robbing and terrorizing the people of Oregon for over ten years. *I bet there's a parcel of reward money on him*, I thought.

A loud crash and bang brought me back to reality when some of the hoodlums began breaking open the cases of goods, amidst much hootin' and hollerin'. I took the opportunity to start slipping on my wet clothes and boots, hoping to go unnoticed.

"Hold on there old-timer. I know who you are. You're Rogue River Roy, a tricky customer as I recall. You just stay in that red union suit so we can keep an eye on you," Whispering Will hissed.

"Yeah, he turned in my cousin over in Grants Pass and the sheriff hung'em," one of the outlaws chimed in. "I ought to gut-shoot 'em right here and leave him for the buzzards. Come to think of it, I ain't seen any buzzards."

"You'll do no such thing, Slim. I got a plan to steal all the gold from that new mine and this old-timer is gonna be a part of it."

*   *   *

Meanwhile, Black Cloud moved silently through the brush to a place where he could hear everything the bad man said. *So that's their game, they're going to rob everybody at the new diggings.* He watched as the men busted open the cases of champagne, broke the necks off the bottles and started to drink the white foaming wine till it bubbled out their noses.

As he knelt in the concealment of the huckleberry bushes, he summed up his predicament. He had to warn the miners, free Rogue River Roy and put on some clothes. Roy was in the greatest danger, so that was his first task. Then he would warn the miners. A plan began to form in his mind and he smiled as he visualized the possibilities.

Black Cloud reentered the small creek and moved downstream slowly and silently till he discovered a clay bank. He searched a nearby gravel bar for a suitable flat rock to dig the clay and was fortunate enough to find a large piece of flint. The old Indian quickly knapped out a cutting edge on one side and started digging, placing the clay on a piece of cedar bark.

Next, Black Cloud walked through the forest till he found several tall fir trees covered with poison oak vines. Those vines were a hundred feet high, growing up the trunks of the trees. Then, he set about covering his body with the clay he had brought with him on the bark carrier. The clay would protect him from the poisonous white sap that dripped from the cut ends of the dangerous vines. Then he used his newly-made tool to cut through the vines at the base of the trees. He began to pull them off in long sections and then he laid the vines in a long bundle, tied the ends together and started off through the woods pulling his unusual cordage.

About a quarter mile down the trail from where the outlaws were holding Roy, Black Cloud started building his trap. It was a big funnel-shaped affair, complete with dead fall and pull cord. The wrinkled old Indian's face split into a big smile as he thought about what was going to happen to that gang of cutthroats.

*   *   *

Soon it was dark and the outlaws built a large fire. They were all gathered around the fire, cavorting and shouting. I sat with my back against a tree and watched those hoodlums drinking up my customers' wine, while they danced around in fancy dresses, laughing and shouting. I sure was glad I didn't drink and make a fool of myself like these bone-heads did, but then bandits never were very smart.

I noticed one of the mules nosing around the broken cases and starting to lick up the creamy contents from one of the broken jars. Before I could say anything, that mule started to disappear . . . ! Right before my very eyes . . . from the head down! Soon she had totally disappeared, every bit of her except her iron shoes. Now, if that wasn't a sight, mule shoes walking around without any mule in 'em. I smiled in spite of my predicament. I'd never seen anything like it. Soon the iron shoes just kinda wandered off up the trail without the rowdy gang even noticing.

The fellow who was assigned to guard me kept starting to nod off, but then he would pop his head back up, look around and then nod off again. I pretended to go to sleep so he wouldn't see me watching him every time his head snapped up. Soon his chin just rested on his chest and he started to snore softly. Now was my chance to see what was in one of those big, white, glass jars that Ruby had licked up. My feet and hands were still tied, so I had to kinda scoot over on my backside to where the container lay. I nosed it over so I could read the label: CRE'ME LE DISPARATRE. It didn't mean anything to me, but maybe Black Cloud would know. (Black Cloud had been schooled by French Missionaries and he could read and write French and English better than most of the settlers.)

At that very moment, Black Cloud was watching the events unfold around the campfire, observing the shadows of the bad men cast against the night by the flames. Suddenly, he felt something pressed against his back. He froze with fear. He had been caught! Then it licked him!

He turned around, but there was nothing there! The hair on the back of his neck stood up and goose-bumps covered his body under the dark gray clay. This was strange, very strange. Then he noticed the four mule shoes in the dim light. He reached out to pick up one just as Ruby moved her hoof.

"Oooohhhh!" he yelped when she kicked him by accident. He recovered his courage and looked to see if any of the bandits had heard him. They were making so much noise in their merriment, you could have fired a cannon and they wouldn't have noticed.

He saw Rogue River Roy lying on his belly looking real close at some white object. He picked up a small pebble and tossed it at Roy. It hit him on the leg. Roy jumped and then squinted into the night. Black Cloud threw another pebble a little short so Roy could see the direction it came from. At that, Roy picked up one of the unbroken jars and tossed it two-handed in the general direction of Black Cloud. It landed near the Indian, who picked it up and held it to the dancing firelight. French words were imprinted on the object saying it was disappearing cream and to use it sparingly. He chuckled to himself and said softly to the mule, "You must be one big wrinkle old girl, 'cause all of you disappeared."

Black Cloud began to devise a new plan and boy, was it a good one. His body was still covered with clay and he was all but invisible in the darkness. First, he went to the creek and washed off the clay from his head. He squashed a dried blackberry in the middle of his forehead so it would look like a bullet hole. Next, he led the four mule shoes up the trail a little and then mounted and stood on Ruby's back, as she slowly walked towards the fire.

It took a few minutes for the first badman to spot the "dead" Indian's head floating about eight feet in the air. He screamed like the coward he was and started pointing and yelling, "Ghost! . . . Ghost! . . . Ghost!"

Soon they all saw him. Most of them couldn't talk. They were scared speechless. All they could do was stare at the head with the bullet hole in it. Finally, one of them said in a shaky, whispered voice, "What do you want, Indian?"

The eyes in the floating head popped open and a voice boomed: "Your lives!"

With that, the whole gang fled down the trail as fast as they could run. Each one was trying his best not to be last. Some even ran through the fire in their haste, causing sparks to fly everywhere. The floating head made a loud, mournful cry as it chased those desperadoes into the night.

As you might have suspected, they all ended up in a big jumbled ball in a net made from poison oak vines. They dangled high above the forest floor, screaming, "Don't let the ghost get me! Don't let the ghost get me!"

Now, one of the treatments for poison oak is the use of mud to cover the blistering, itching areas of skin, so Black Cloud and I made them throw down their six-shooters in exchange for a little mud before we would lower them to the ground.

It was a strange parade that entered the mining camp the next day. A couple of old muleskinners leading six desperadoes stark naked and covered with mud, with hands tied to their saddle horns and feet tied under their horses. All of them were gagged with their own bandanas so we didn't have to listen to all the whining. Last in line were two pack mules who were loaded down, but real clean and smelling unusually nice.

Black Cloud and I had a lot of explaining to do and when we got to the part where Black Cloud was standing on top of the mule talking from his ghostly head, everyone was laughing so hard they had tears in their eyes and could hardly stand up or catch their breath.

When things settled down, we unpacked the goods. The fancy ladies were very angry about their dresses having been worn briefly by banditos, but the dresses were a little dirty and could easily be made as good as new. As for the champagne, three cases remained. Most of the soap and other ladies' stuff were still alright. I offered to pay for the soap and CRE'ME LE DISPARATRE we had used, but they all agreed that we had probably saved all the gold in camp and many lives to boot, so they called it even.

About a week later, Black Cloud and I caused another ruckus when we rode into Grants Pass down Main Street headed for Sheriff Ketchem's jail. The sheriff was flabbergasted by what he saw: six wanted outlaws who were covered with cracking dry mud and squirming in their saddles trying to scratch.

"Hello Roy. Howdy Black Cloud. Looks like you hit the jackpot this time. Is that who I think it is?" The sheriff smiled. He untied one of the mounted men and hauled him to the ground, then rubbed his neck. "Do you know who this is, Roy? It's Whispering Will. I got a pile of Wanted Posters on him alone. Well, I'll be darned."

A few days later, Black Cloud and I were at the telegraph office collecting our reward money when I asked him if he was going to buy Dancing Flower a present and spend a little time at home. He thought for a while and then said, "Maybe I'll just mosey on up north. I hear they got a smoking mountain that glows at night. I'd like to see that before I go to the Happy Hunting Ground."

I was shocked. "Aren't you feeling well, old friend?"

"No! No! Nothing like that. I'm going to Agness to hunt deer this fall so I can make some real good jerky."

"Maybe I'll see you there."

In fact, I had a feeling I couldn't avoid it.

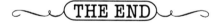

THE END

That wasn't really the end, because the end was when I got to Agness that fall a little ahead of Black Cloud. I saw him walking along the trail leading uphill and away from the river. I put my plan into action! First, I placed four mule-shoes – complete with nails poking through them – spaced out on the path,

as if a mule was standing
there. Then, I laid a broken twig under one of the
shoes. I found a similar-
sized branch and hid in
the brush besides the
trail.

When Black Cloud
was about ten feet from
the shoes, I snapped the
twig I held in my hands.
I was shaking with sup-
pressed laughter as he
froze in his tracks. See-

ing the shoes, Black Cloud looked
around, then took a few steps forward and said softly,
"Is that you, Ruby?"

Silence filled the air.

"It's me, your old friend Black Cloud," as he
walked closer to the four mule-shoes on the ground.
Then he reached out with his hand to find the mule's
head so he could pat her.

I couldn't contain myself any longer. I stumbled
out of the bushes with tears in my eyes, hardly able
to see. I was laughing so hard I fell to the ground and
held my stomach as I hooted with glee. I began to
imitate him: "Is that you, Ruby?" This was followed
by further convulsions of laughter.

Black Cloud started to laugh, too. He knew he
had been had by an expert and he realized how funny
he must've looked standing there reaching out for a

mule that didn't exist.

We made camp together that night and Black Cloud whipped up a batch of my biscuits and fried some bacon for supper. I only woke up three times during the night laughing – "Is that you Ruby?" I wasn't one to rub in a joke!

Now *this* is...

THE END!

TALE THIRTEEN
THE GREAT SHOOT-OUT IN GOLD BEACH

The year was 1889 and in October there was gonna be a shoot-out. Every year when hunting season rolled around, most hunters would "sight in" their rifles. Now, whenever a bunch of good old boys got together, there'd be a lot of bragging about who was the best shot. There was usually more talkin' than shootin' and talkin' don't put meat on the table.

This year was going to be different. The Outdoor Store put up a fifty-dollar prize to be given to the winner of the shoot-off. Then everyone would know for sure who the best shot in Curry County was. There was a fifty-cent entry fee and that was a lot of money. Back then you could buy a good rifle for eleven dollars, with a box of shells thrown in.

Scotty MacFrugal was the thriftiest man who ever lived on the Rogue River. WASTE NOT, WANT NOT was the motto on his family crest, but we never saw it because he was to cheap pay the postage to get one.

MacFrugal read the handbill the store had printed up about the contest and the part about the fifty-dollar prize really got his attention. He was an excellent rifle shot, but his old rifle was so worn out that the bullets just tumbled out of the barrel. He knew he had to have a new rifle if he was going to have a chance at winning. So, he headed over to the Outdoor Store to look over the available rifles and check on who had entered the contest so far. There were about thirty shooters already signed up and he read the list carefully: Coos Bay Bob, H. Jones, Mayor Cannon, Rick O'Shay, Siskiyou Sam, Tall Bill, Sergeant Dutch, Rogue River Roy, M. T. Pockets, I. M. Wilds, and Big Tim. They were some of the better shooters listed so far. He absolutely would have to have a new rifle if he was going to compete with that crowd.

They had a fine collection of firearms for sale: a Ballard, Winchesters, Sharps and a Marlin – it would be hard to choose. MacFrugal took a long time looking them over. He must've stood there an hour. He wanted a good rifle, but he just hated to part with the money. When another hour went by, Handsome Jim, the proprietor, was getting a little impatient and he reached under the counter and pulled out a rifle he had bought off a guide the day before.

Mike, the guide, had found this particular rifle in the river – it had probably been lost by some greenhorn from back East when his canoe flipped over. It needed a little cleaning, but it appeared to be in excellent condition. The price was nine dollars. MacFrugal looked it over and discovered it was a No. 3 Remington-Hepburn Long Range Creedmoor Rifle, a target rifle, exactly what he needed. He was so excited that he said "I'll take it" without even bargaining for a box of shells to be thrown in. It was very unusual for a man as thrifty as MacFrugal to be so impulsive. With trembling hands, he pulled out his seldom-seen pocket purse. It was one of those folded leather ones with a double snap on top. It squeaked mournfully like a bagpipe when he opened it.

Scotty dumped all the coins on the counter and painfully counted out the nine dollars, with an extra fifty cents for the entry fee. All the coins seemed a little larger than normal; it was probably the way he squeezed the most out of them.

Jim handed him the rifle, then turned and picked up a box of shells saying, "I guess you'll need these, too." A strange look appeared on Scotty's face, until Jim said, "I'll throw the ammo in for free." MacFrugal smiled with relief, thanked him, and headed for the range with his new rifle.

I happened to be walking past the store with my mule train when Scotty came out carrying his new rifle. I listened to his story and looked at the rifle. But when I asked Mc Frugal how much he paid for it, he didn't answer. I thought maybe he didn't hear me, so I repeated the question. MacFrugal told me it "hurt his lips" to say the amount and he would tell me when it wasn't quite so painful.

I let Scotty know that the new type shells he

would be using in his rifle could be reloaded and that he could save some money and get more accuracy. The save money part got him interested real fast and he asked me to tell him all about it. So I sat down right there in the road and talked for two hours about the finer points of reloading. MacFrugal was hooked. He started the very next day using borrowed equipment and powder I loaned him.

Now, if we're going to talk about people that get the utmost out of everything they use, then MacFrugal was King. He could absolutely wring the most good out of anything he put his mind to. He borrowed a book on ballistics and did some very close, accurate calculations in order to come up with the perfect quantity of powder – not too much and not too little. MacFrugal weighed the powder out on a scale he had made himself. It wasn't as accurate as it was repeatable however and repeatability is the secret to successful shooting.

He cleaned his new rifle thoroughly and then fired three rounds to check the grouping of his shots. It was the best he had ever seen and now he was on a "quest for the best." He borrowed books on shooting skills and then started experimenting with what he had learned. In a few days, he had obtained excellent results and was ready for the shoot-off.

The day of the contest, the town was crowded with shooters and hunters from all over Southern Oregon. Some even came over the mountains from Grants Pass and Roseburg. They were a tough, rowdy bunch, but a friendly spirit filled the air. There were contestants from Squaw Valley, Ophir, Port Orford, Langlois, Brookings, Jerry's Flat, Agness, Coos Bay and Bandon, to mention a few places.

When Big Tim from Sixes, Oregon walked into town, all eyes turned to greet him. He waved a cheerful hello to his many friends. His blue eyes had a confident look, as only a man sure of his skills could give. Big Tim was a friendly sort and when he smiled, everyone smiled. But when it came to shooting, he was deadly serious and everyone else was serious, too. Tim carried a heavy-barreled rifle that looked like it was made from a wagon axle. His powers with it were legendary.

BANG . . . ! A revolver went off and everybody froze. Not a sound was heard as everyone looked for the source of the explosion. It was Jim, shooting his revolver on the steps of the Outdoor Store to let everyone know to line up so he could count them and give instructions about the match.

First of all, there would be no drinking during the shoot-off, because drinkin' and shootin' don't mix. Next, he counted all the contestants; a hundred and sixty-eight shooters had shown up – many more than had been expected. He divided the men into fourteen groups by lottery. The winner of each group would be in the final shoot-out.

Earlier, Jim had set up targets on the beach. The contestants shot all morning, eliminating all but the final three. It came down to Big Tim, Scotty MacFrugal, and Rogue River Roy. They were deadlocked with perfect scores.

Now, the most remarkable thing that these shooters had ever seen was when they examined MacFrugal's paper target and found out that his bullets had only gone *halfway* through the paper! The bullets just hung there, right in the center of the paper. When asked about it, he said, "I dinna wanna waste me powder. Ye need only enough to do the job an not a dram more."

The three finalists had everyone's total attention, as they stepped up to the firing line and loaded their rifles. The wind started to blow, as it often does in the afternoon on the Oregon Coast. Big Tim had an uncanny ability to shoot in all types of weather, a skill he had learned during his many years of hunting. The heavy barrel also helped in steadying his aim.

I was wearing my signature red and black-checkered shirt. I was more of a "fair weather" shooter, but was probably the most accurate of the three. In pistol shooting, I was the best in three counties, but this wasn't pistol shooting. Scotty MacFrugal had the best rifle, but not the instincts of the other two shooters, nor the experience.

They shot three more times and it was still a tie. The wind was blowing at least thirty knots, when Tim said, "Let's end this nonsense. Do you see that rabbit down on the beach by that big log?" All eyes turned in unison and looked towards the log that must've been six hundred yards away. A murmur went through the crowd. None of them could see the rabbit. I said, "You mean the one facing this way in the grass?"

"Yup," said Big Tim. "That's the one. You take the left ear and I'll take the right."

"What will I take?" said Scotty MacFrugal.

"You'll take the prize if we both miss, Mac," Tim said.

Scotty thought it over – it was an impossible shot. No one in the world could shoot across a thirty-knot wind at six hundred yards – it was nearly a third of a mile! He nodded his head in acceptance.

Both I and Big Tim adjusted the rear sights on our rifles and stepped up to the firing line. A hush fell over the boisterous crowd. The wind tugged at their clothing and buffeted their long guns. They took careful aim and fired simultaneously, as the wind gusted to thirty-five knots. The report was deafening.

Some of those in the crowd started to run down to the big log, but Big Tim stopped them, saying, "Let MacFrugal go alone. He's the one who's got the most to lose." They all stopped dead in their tracks. When Big Tim spoke, everyone listened.

Mac arrived at the log about ten minutes later and was very surprised at what he found: an old driftwood log, gray with age. There were two fresh bullet holes within six inches of a large knot hole . . . ! These shooters were not to be trifled with. Below the log was a small, covered basket hidden in the beach grass. Scotty opened it very carefully. As he suspected, there was a little rabbit with a tiny nick on each ear and a note inside the lid that said simply, "A third of something is better than all of nothing." Scotty put the fuzzy, little critter in his hat and headed back to the crowd.

As he walked, he tried to figure out what had happened. Then it came to him – Roy and Tim must've placed the rabbit in the basket early that morning. If they tied, as they usually did, Tim would suggest this was an absolutely impossible shot and it would

be a grand joke on all of them. After all, they won the shooting contest fair and square. This was just a little extra fun they were having. During shoot-offs, they always shot after he did and duplicated his shots, causing a three-way tie.

Now, wait a minute! How many times had these two characters pulled jokes like this? From now on they should be watched more closely. When he got back to the waiting crowd and the other shooters, he pulled the rabbit out of his hat and pointed to the notches at the end of its ears. They all looked at the little guy in stunned silence and shook their heads in disbelief. Then all at once they cheered and carried me and Tim on their shoulders into the town watering hole for refreshments.

It went down in history as the best simultaneous shots ever fired on the Rogue River. It was also the greatest joke ever played on the shooters of the South Coast. It became known as "the hat trick."

The next morning, MacFrugal found sixteen dollars and sixty-seven cents in his boot. It wasn't fifty dollars, but it would help buy feed for his new pet rabbit, who he had named *Notch*. In years to come, whenever he ran into those other shooters, there would be a wink and a nod. It was their private joke.

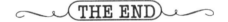

THE END

TALE FOURTEEN

THE FASTEST GUNPOWDER IN THE WEST

I've heard many stories about fast guns in the Old West, but never one about fast gunpowder. I feel obligated to tell this tale about Scotty MacFrugal as it really happened. The year was 1892, July Fourth to be exact. An old-timer by the name of Scotty MacFrugal – a thriftier man never lived – had started to do some reloading for his new rifle. Now, this really started because he wanted to win some money in The Great South Coast Shoot-Off, back in '89.

Well, sir, he caught on so fast and was so crafty (Cheap) that he ended up in a three-way tie for first place with Big Tim and me. Now, that's a whole different story about accuracy and a little trickery. This tale's about fast powder. One thing I have to tell you first, though, is that he measured his powder so close that when the judges checked the targets, they found the bullets halfway through the heavy paper. What a sight it was! If you don't believe me, I can show you the targets.

I'd better get on with my story . . . Oh! Just one other thing to show you how creative (Cheap) MacFrugal was: when he got the contract to paint the old Curry County Court House some ugly, mud-green color, his bid was lower than the County Commissioner's nephew. They furnished him twenty gallons of paint. The first thing he did was to take eighteen of them back to Dan's Hardware Store and pocket the money. Then he painted the entire Court House with two coats.

Everyone thought it was remarkable to be so conservative (Cheap) and still do such a good job. But the surprising thing was that his boat turned up the same color, then his wagon, then his house, then his fence and finally, his barn. Now, that's what I call Frugal! And that's also how the word was coined.

When Scotty MacFrugal first came to Gold Beach back in '76, he had with him a keg of black powder that he had bought off an Indian scout, who had bought it off a French sergeant from Montreal, who had stole it from a muleskinner from Kentucky, and Lord knows where he got it. It was a very special powder. It was bright blue! Now, I know it couldn't be blue and still be called black powder, but I seen it and you'll just have to trust me.

MacFrugal had that blue powder stored out in his barn for years and never tried any of it. Then one day he ran low on black powder and was going to head out for the Outdoor Store, when he remembered that old keg up in the rafters. He hated to part with the money for a new keg of powder, so he got down that old keg and popped out the bung. When he poured a little into a jar lid and touched it off with a match, it flashed so brightly that all he could see for ten minutes was a bright white ball. He thought, *this is quite vigorous, I best proceed cautiously.*

MacFrugal had purchased a very expensive used rifle to use in the Great South Coast Shoot-Off of '89: a No.3 Remington-Hepburn Long-Range Creedmore. A finer rifle was never made and he got it dirt cheap at the Outdoor Store. It was such a fine rifle that he didn't want to risk it with the old blue powder while he was trying to work-up a load. His old Winchester rifle was so worn out that the bullets just tumbled down the barrel, so he thought he'd test the blue powder using the Winchester. Well, it's a darn good thing he did, because even with a half-charge, he still managed to blow the rifle apart. Fortunately, he had the Winchester in a vice in the barn and pulled the trigger with a string. Scotty MacFrugal was cautious as well as economical (Cheap).

Next, he made some careful calculations and did something you are never supposed to do: he mixed some blue powder with some black! I can't tell you the proportions, because he kept it all a big secret, but I can tell you this: he started with just a little blue and keep on increasing the amount till he almost got what he wanted.

Photography was just getting popular and they used a pan of silver powder that ignited as they took the picture. *It was a regular flash in the pan.* Now, this silver stuff was really fast burning powder. I guess you know what's coming next! Scotty started a three-way mix: a little black, a little blue and a little silver. He tried every combination you could imagine.

At first, it was just a little better than regular powder, but then it started getting faster and faster and faster and soon it was so fast that the bullet hole appeared in the target just *before* he pulled the trigger!

Now, that's fast!

THE END

TALE FIFTEEN
POKEY

Now, I've been skinning mules for over fifty years and I've seen some mighty big mules, some as big as Clydesdales. I've also seen some mighty small ones, some as small as a St. Bernard. But I've never seen one as slow as Pokey. He was so slow you'd have to drive a stake alongside of him to see if he was moving at all. Normally, I'd have traded him off, but he was the offspring of Fast Fanny, a mule that had once saved my life –but that's a whole different story.

My patience was drawing thin with that slow mule, but the last straw was when I was taking him on his first pack trip all the way to Grants Pass from Gold Beach. We were off at the crack of dawn. Now, I can usually tell when it's dawn by looking at my old shirt hanging on a nail near my bed. When I can tell it's checkered, it's time to get up and get moving.

We hit the trail and walked till the sun was high overhead. I figured it was lunchtime and thought

I'd build a little fire and cook some beans. When I looked around I discovered we were still in the front yard! So I just walked back to the cook house and ate there.

At the end of the third day I was still able to turn around and see the bunk-house – and this was a small spread. On the fourth day we came to the barbed wire that marked the property line. This would never do. I was going to have to get rid of Pokey.

About three years ago, a neighbor and *former* friend had traded me a fine-looking black stallion for two plow horses. When I went to take a look at the stallion, I noticed an old gray mare that was so sway-back its belly nearly touched the ground. She was off in a pasture by herself and I never gave her another thought. Well, we made the deal and I was to bring the two plow horses over that evening and pick up the black stallion. I arrived just before dark and Mr. Delbert Fraud invited me in for a glass of hard cider, which I never refuse.

By the time I left his ranch house, it was pitch black, so he led me out to the hitching post and handed me the reins to my new horse. We shook hands on our agreement and I strode off into the darkness leading my new steed. I trusted D. Fraud completely – after all he was a former lawyer from Fresno, California.

The next morning when I went out to the barn to feed and admire the new horse ... what did I see in the stall? That old swayback nag! I was furious! I returned to the house and slapped on my rig, rotated the cylinders, checked for caps on both revolvers, and stormed out the door.

As I approached the Fraud spread, I could see two people on the front porch in a couple of rocking chairs. Delbert Fraud was in one and Sheriff Sam Slammer was in the other. Delbert saw the expression on my face as I bounded up the steps. "I don't want any trouble, Roy. A deal is a deal. So I'm asking Sheriff Slammer to escort you off my property."

I was angry. I was speechless. My face must've been the color of a fall apple.

"Now, hold on there, Roy," said the sheriff. "I'd like to ask you a few questions. Did you shake hands on the trade when Mr. Fraud handed you the reins to the horse in question?"

"Yes, but it was the wrong . . . ."

"No buts about it, Roy, you shook hands. A deal's a deal. That's the way I see it. I'm going to escort you off Mr. Fraud's ranch and I don't want any trouble."

Well, that little swindle had stuck in my craw for three years now and it was return the favor to that low down, @#$%^&*, miserable sidewinder. I still get hot under the collar just thinking

about it.

Over the past few years, I've had occasion to talk with most of the neighbors and found all of them have been cheated by that shifty-eyed D. Fraud. Every one of them was seeking revenge. They would help me if I came up with a plan, but only if it was a lowdown sneaky, rotten, cheating, vile, stinking one. It sure was nice to have such thoughtful friends. In fact, Mr. Fraud acquired his property from John McCormick about five years ago on a rigged bet. Fraud cheated McCormick in a horse race using twin stallions ridden by the Duplicity Brothers. McCormick still lived in town, alone and always dreaming about the family spread he had lost. The only reason the secret got out about the sham race was the fact that the Duplicity Brothers got drunk one night down at the Green Lantern Saloon and bragged about it. They told how one of them had hidden in the bushes on the return leg of the race and rode out on a fresh horse just as Old John went by. He overtook McCormick on the fresh horse and won the race.

* * *

I had about twenty acres that I put into oats every spring. Some of the crop was for my mules and the rest I sold to my customers and friends. I owned some real fertile ground just over the hill towards the entrance to my small ranch. It was the centerpiece of my *plan* to exact revenge on Fraud with a little help from the other ranchers and farmers, who had been told where to go, what to bring, when to do it and to do it quietly.

I arrived at the Fraud ranch early one spring day and was greeted by a double-barreled shotgun when I pounded on the front door.

"Now, hold on there, Delbert, this is a friendly visit. Let's just let bygones be bygones. No reason for two grown men to be on the outs over some little mis-understanding."

He opened the door all the way and leaned his shotgun against the jam. He came cautiously out onto the porch and looked at me real close to see if he could determine any deception in my manner. Evidently he must've been convinced, because he left the handiness of the scatter gun and offered me a rocker to sit in.

We talked for about an hour and then I invited him over to my house for a cup of the hard cider that we put up last fall. I heard him smack his lips – he was a fool for good hard cider.

He saddled up his fine black stallion; I hopped on my old mule Ruby; and we took off for the ranch. As we approached my spread, I drew my Colt .44 and fired a shot, aiming way down the road. After we had ridden for about five minutes, I dismounted and picked up a jackrabbit, tied his ears together and hung him on my saddle horn. As I remounted, Delbert exclaimed, "That was the most fantastic shot I've ever seen. Why it must've been four hundred yards!"

"More like five hundred," I said. "But I was aiming for his head and only hit him in the neck."

.

Little did he know I had placed the rabbit on the trail that very morning, but much more than that, the shot was the signal to all the neighbors to put the PLAN into action.

My nephew Matt was out in the oat patch harnessing up Pokey to start the spring plowing. I called out to him, "If you finish by noon, we'll go fishing down to Secret Bar and try to catch that old lunker."

"I'll do my best Uncle Roy – I bet I can catch that old fish."

"Do you think he can?" said Mr. Fraud.

"Sure, he's developing into a mighty fine fisherman."

"No! No! Can he plow that big field before noon?" Fraud was getting excited.

"Well, he should – he's using old Pokey."

I tried to change the subject all the way back to the bunkhouse, but Delbert wouldn't let go of it. He was like a bull dog with a bone. He kept asking about the mule and I kept avoiding his questions.

Finally he said, "I'll bet you five hundred dollars that he can't get that field plowed by noon."

When we got closer to the house, I could see someone sitting on the front porch with his chair leaned back on its hind legs. The glint of a knife showed as he whittled on a maple branch. *Probably making a whistle*, I thought. As he rocked forward, I saw the flash of his badge and knew it was Sheriff Slammer.

"Howdy Sheriff. What brings you to this bend of the river?"

"I just happened to be out this way and thought I'd drop in and see how you're doing. You didn't catch that big lunker, did you?"

"No, not yet, but I'm sure young Matt will get a line on him. Why don't you step inside and have a glass of cider while I put up this old mule?"

We settled in the front room to drink cider. The sheriff wanted to talk fishing and Delbert wanted to bet on the plowing of the oat field. The longer we sat there, the more flustered Delbert became. He really wanted to bet. Finally, he bet me the incredible sum of five thousand dollars that the field would not get plowed by noon. He had just seen my nephew walk by the barn with his fishing pole in one hand and a can of worms in the other, heading for the Rogue River. He knew I hadn't noticed the boy and he thought he was betting on a sure thing.

Five thousand dollars was a lot of money back then – why it could buy five ranches just like this one. I sprung out of my chair and shook Delbert's hand before he could say another word. "It's a deal, Del."

I looked over at the sheriff just as Fraud shouted, "Did you see that sheriff? We shook hands on it. Now it's legal." He rubbed his hands together as if he was already counting my money.

Little did Fraud know that the neighbors had brought twenty teams of mules and horses, and plowed that oat field while we were sitting and drinking hard cider! They had been hiding in the alder grove below the field when we rode past. My shot at the rabbit was a warning to be quiet and get ready to bring all the plow teams to the field after we were out of earshot.

They had a wagon loaded with planks to walk the animals to the field so they wouldn't leave any tracks. Each one of them plowed a small section of the field and then walked 'em out on the planks, so as not to leave a trace. They left Pokey at the end of the field all covered with dirt and still harnessed to a plow.

We ate dinner; the sheriff talked fishing; and Del squirmed. When we were finished, he bolted for the door and was on his horse even before the sheriff and I pushed back our chairs.

When we crested the hill, Delbert Fraud was already there shaking his head with tears in his eyes and saying, "I just can't believe it. I just can't believe it."

Sure enough, the whole field was plowed with nice, neat furrows. Pokey was standing at the end of the field still hitched to the plow. The old gray, sway-back horse was alongside, nosing up to the mule. Matt was nowhere to be seen.

"I've never seen the like," said the sheriff. "The whole field's plowed and that mule hasn't even broken a sweat. Well, I do declare."

Just then, Matt came walking out of the alder trees with something wrapped in a large skunk cabbage leaf. He walked up to us with greetings to everyone and then laid the bundle at our feet. When he opened it up, there lay one of the biggest trout I had ever seen. A real lunker. I don't think I'd ever seen Sheriff Slammer so excited. He kneeled down, picked up the fish. "I'll bet this one's over fifteen pounds. My, what a fish! What a fish! Congratulations Matt – that's a mighty fine fish."

We were interrupted by Mr. D. Fraud's sobbing, as the full impact of the totally plowed field hit him. The sheriff looked at him and said, "You shook hands on the bet and a deal is a deal. Now pay up! That was five thousand dollars, if I recall. It's lucky for Roy that I was here to witness the wager."

"It was pure luck, sheriff, pure luck." I looked over at Matt and winked.

"I'm real proud of you for catching that old Goliath of a fish, Matt, but I'm very disappointed in you for running off and letting that mule plow the field all by himself."

"Do you mean this mule plows by himself?" Delbert couldn't believe it.

"Yep, he sure does. Why you've seen it yourself, haven't you?" I said.

"Yes, I guess so and by the way how much do you want for that old mule?"

"He's not for sale. He's far too valuable. Now, sheriff, if you will accompany us to the bank in town I'll collect my wager," I said.

Fraud started to protest, but I put up my hand to silence him. We headed for town right away because we wanted to get there before the bank closed.

Let me tell you, five thousand in gold is a parcel of money. I thought it would split the seams in my old saddlebags. I figured if I moved quickly I'd complete my errand before any unsavory characters got a whiff of what was going on. After all I did have my old scatter gun and both six guns to get me out of any trouble I got into.

I visited twenty ranches and farms on the way home and gave each family two hundred and forty dollars. It took me the better part of three days, because they all wanted to hear the story over and over again. Justice is sweet but revenge is delightful.

Before I left each place, I told them about the next step in the PLAN. They all laughed and hooted when they thought about the probable outcome and then sent me merrily on my way. It was hardly dawn, when the banging on the front door woke me from a great fishing dream. "Alright! Alright! I'm coming! Keep your shirt on!" I shuffled into my clothes and headed for the door. " Who is it?" I said, sliding my shotgun off its pegs.

"It's me, your friend Delbert Fraud. Open up; I have to talk to you."

He pushed in as soon as the door started to move. "I just got to have that mule! I haven't sleep for three nights thinking about it."

"Good morning, neighbor." I lit the hurricane lamp and lowered the chimney. "What mule are you talking about?" I inquired innocently.

"You know darn well what mule I talking about. It's that Pokey. I've got to have him! I'll give you a hundred dollars for him!"

Now, a hundred dollars for a ten-dollar mule

is a pretty good deal, so I told him, "I'm really not interested in selling him. He's like one of the family – why I'd as soon sell my nephew."

"O. K.! I'll give you two hundred dollars and not a penny more."

"Now, calm down, Del. That old mule isn't worth that much. After you think it over, you'll probably want your money back."

"No! No! I'd never do that. I'll sign a paper, anything, just sell me that confounded mule." He was actually whining!

"If you got your heart set on it, we'll go to town today and let the sheriff witness the transaction – but the price is four hundred dollars."

"Whatever you say, friend and thank you, thank you very much." He seemed quite relieved.

Evidently, he had seen the poster about the state plowing contest and the one thousand dollar prize for First Place. Even Governor Fencestradler would be there to hand out the trophy and the cash, one thousand dollars in gold coin. With enough side bets, this would be a great opportunity for Mr. Fraud to recover his losses and possibly launch his political career. He had all the qualifications, as I saw it. Without any moral values to hold him back, devoid of compassion for his fellow man and an all-consuming desire for wealth and power, he was the perfect candidate!

We went to town and completed our business in front of Sheriff Slammer, with the agreement I would drop off old Pokey the next day by wagon. I delivered the mule as agreed upon without incident and returned to my ranch.

We were out by the corral mending some sagging fence, when I noticed a cloud of dust heading our way. I looked over at Matt and said, "I wonder who that could be in such an all-fired hurry?"

He smiled and winked. "Gee, I couldn't even guess."

We starting laughing and barely got the smiles off our faces as Mr. Fraud reigned up his fine stallion in a cloud of dust. He leaped off his horse and suddenly we were nose to nose and he was screaming that I was a liar and a cheat and he wanted his money back.

"Now, hold on, neighbor. You best back off or loosen your hammer thong if you're going to talk that kinda talk." I stood on my toes and moved even closer to him for effect. He quieted down some and started to tell me what happened.

"I hooked that Pokey mule up to a plow and when I came back about an hour latter he hadn't moved at all. I want my money back right now." Del was shouting at the top of his lungs.

"Now hold on Fraud. Do you remember I told you that mule wasn't worth the money and you would probably want your money back?"

"Err . . . , err . . . , yes I do." He stammered.

"O. K. But let me explain the problem. Do you recall the old mare that was at the end of the field when Pokey plowed the twenty acres?"

"Well kind'a."

"That's it," I explained. "Pokey has to have that sweet old horse at the end of the field or he won't hit a lick. He really likes that old nag for some reason."

'So you're trying to tell me the mule is worthless without that old gray, swayback nag?"

"You got it. I must've failed to tell you before."

He pondered a moment, then said, "How much do you want for that old, swayback, good-for-nothing, holdout from the glue factory?"

"Well, I've grown quite attached to her and really don't want to part with her, so . . . ."

"Let's get to it. What's it going to take for me to get that old nag back to my ranch with me?"

* * *

Delbert Fraud sure did look funny riding that old gray mare with his feet dragging on the ground. Even the silver-studded saddle looked a little out-of-place.

Matt just beamed as he looked over his new black stallion. He was getting him ready to ride out to tell the neighbors to put the second half of the PLAN into action.

"Don't forget the coyote and the red ribbon," I reminded him.

As for me, I took off for the Fraud place to "help" Delbert. When I rode up to the main house, I could see him out in a field hitching Pokey to a large plow.

"Hello neighbor. Did you realize today is the last day to sign-up for the plowing contest?" He looked up with a blank expression on his face. Quite obviously he had totally forgotten, what with all the other things going wrong.

"I'm heading for town to sign-up. If you've a mind to, you can come along with me."

What about the mule and the plowing?" Fraud said.

"Don't worry about it. Just put that old gray horse at the end of the field and everything will be O. K."

"All right; give me a minute to saddle up and I'll be right with you."

When he came out of the barn, he was leading a fine-looking sorrel mare that must've been a recent purchase. Now, that's a very fine horse, I thought to myself.

We rode for about half an hour and he started talking about the shot I had taken at that jackrabbit a few days ago. He bet I could never duplicate it.

I told him it all depended on your eyes. If you can see it, you can hit it. I asked him how his eyes were and he said he had superior eyes, as he was a superior person. So that was it - he was tall, good-looking, intelligent, and thought he was better than anyone else. He used people, took advantage of his friends, and thought it was his right to do so.

Then I noticed a little piece of red cloth tied low on a bush just off the trail. I reigned up Ruby. "Do you see that mangy coyote down the trail about six hundred yards?" I said.

"Where?" He looked puzzled.

"Right there – he slipped under that barbed wire and left a little tuft of fur on it." I pointed at the fence. "Now he's looking this way."

"Oh yes! I see him now," he said, but I knew he was lying.

I smiled. D. Fraud couldn't admit someone else might have better eyesight than he had – after all he was the superior man.

"Tell you what," he said. "I'll bet you a hundred dollars you can't hit him from here."

I was silent for a long time and then said, "I only have enough money to pay the contest fee and a little leftover for a piece of Apple Pie and a glass of milk at the Port Hole Restaurant. I never bet more than I have on me, so I guess we'll have to forget the bet. I'll just go ahead and take my shot."

"Now, hold on there, Roy. You do have something of value and you're riding it."

"Oh! I could never bet my favorite mule on a long shot like that. It's too risky, what with the wind and all.

"What's the matter old-timer, losing your nerve, afraid to bet on a little pistol shot?" He was well known for taunting others.

"Alright, but I'm going to dismount and put my back against that tan oak, or it's no bet – if that's fair enough with you."

"Take your shot, Roy. It's a bet."

I dismounted and walked over and shook Delbert's hand, then sat down with my back pressed against the oak tree. I broke off a little tuft of dry grass and let it fall in the steady breeze. Then I braced my forearms on my knees, took long, careful aim, and squeezed the trigger. BANG! . . . BANG!

"Why'd you take two shots, Roy?"

"Well, the first one was going to hit him in the left ear, so I fired again to hit him in the head. You always want a clean shot," I said.

We rode awhile, with Del up ahead and after going about six hundred yards, he stopped and said. "I guess you missed him, Roy. Too bad you'll have to walk to town. Now, if you don't mind, get off my mule and hit the trail." He laughed.

"Let's go a little piece more, Delbert, I'm sure I hit him."

"I'll give you another five minutes and then you'll have to get off my mule old-timer. @#$%&*, he said. Mr. Fraud had evidentially spotted the coyote up ahead.

There was a tuft of fur on the barbed-wire, a bullet hole in the left ear and one in the head. [I noticed two bullet holes in a nearby fence post about three inches apart. That's what I was really aiming at.]

"You see that little spot of white fur on his tail? Well, that's the same ornery critter that killed two of my lambs last spring," I said. "Feel free to ride my horse into town and back, Delbert. I'll pick him up at your place when we return."

"@#$%^&*...*&^%$#@... @#$%^&*," were Fraud's only comments, along with a lot of mumbling about bad luck.

After we paid our entry fees at the court house, I invited him to have a piece of Apple Pie and coffee at the old Port Hole Restaurant. It was the least I could do. I was not only buying the pie, I was buying some time.

When we had finished our delicious Apple Pie and coffee, I told Fraud to ride on ahead and I would catch up with him, as I had a few errands to do. Next, I stopped at Fergy's Men's Store and picked out a real expensive suit of clothes and a hat and boots to match. I told Fergy a gentleman would be coming in to be fitted, but I would pay for them now. I handed him some gold coins and then I paid a visit to John McCormick and told him about the PLAN. He looked older than when I last saw him, it must be his new white mustache and goatee.

I rode Ruby hard and soon caught up with Delbert. He said nothing when I greeted him. He was in a really loathsome mood, but a smile returned to his grumpy face as we came around a bend in the trail and he could see the field all plowed. There was the smell of freshly turned earth on the breeze. Pokey was standing next to the little swayback mare, his legs covered with fresh dirt. He was still hitched to the plow. I looked around and couldn't see a trace of the mules and horses that had *really* plowed the field. I'd have to compliment their owners on the excellent deception.

Delbert hooted with joy, took his hat off, and did a little dance, saying, "I'm going to make me a pack of money betting on you little fella, yes sir, a pack of money." He hardly noticed me drop his saddle on the ground and ride off on Ruby with my new horse in tow.

*   *   *

The plowing contest was being held south of Brookings, the only place in Curry County with enough flat ground to hold such a huge event. A crowd of thousands had arrived to see the contest, get a glimpse of the new Governor and enjoy the carnival-like atmosphere. There were vendors selling food and gadgets and little tents with side shows – it was a very festive affair.

Mr. D. Fraud was circulating though the crowd making bets and shaking hands. He was stopped by an older, well dressed gentleman who made a large bet of five thousand dollars at ten to one odds. That meant if Delbert won, he would win fifty thousand dollars, but if he lost he would have to come up with five thousand dollars or something of equal value. Lucky for him, he spotted Sheriff Slammer talking to me and got him to witness the wager. He looked quiz-zically at the old fellow as if he was somewhat famil-iar, but he evidently couldn't remember where he had seen him before. Fraud must've thought he was very wealthy.

Barroom . . . ! A small cannon going off startled the spectators. It was the signal for the contest to begin. Pokey had been unloaded from the wagon right in place and was all harnessed and ready to go – *or was that ready to stall!*

Just before the signal to begin was given, Delbert Fraud walked up to the reviewing stand and addressed Governor Fencestradler. In his puffy-toad voice, he said so all could hear, "Governor, I'm going to donate my winnings to the Dempublican Party." The Governor replied he was delighted and reached down to shake Del's hand and ask his name.

I'm going to spare you the embarrassing details of the contest . . . . No, I think I will tell. Sometimes it's good to hear about a selfish, lying, cheating, underhanded, blowhard get his comeuppance.

While the rest of the teams charged down the field, Pokey just stood there. D. Fraud yelled and screamed at the poor little mule, all to no avail. Then he pulled out his riding crop and started to whip the helpless creature. I started forward to stop the raging scoundrel, but the Governor was quicker. He was off the stand, through the crowd and grabbing Delbert's arm as it was raised to land another blow. Fraud turned and started to strike his attacker, until he realized it was Governor Fencestradler, himself, that held his arm. He started to apologize, but the damage had been done. He

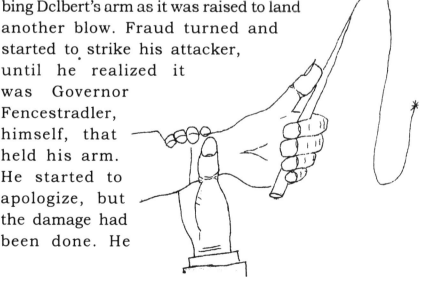

would never have a political career in this state. That was for sure.

To make a short story longer, John McCormick got his ranch back; we all had a good neighbor once again; and Matt got a fine black stallion. I traded Mr. D. Fraud the sorrel mare for Pokey, straight across, just before he left to go back to Fresno, California (which was Punishment enough!).

You don't think I would really trade that that sweet little mule away, do you?

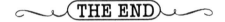

THE END

TALE
SIXTEEN
THE WINTER'S
WOOD FOR 1888

The citizens of Gold Beach gather once a year at the old mill to celebrate and give thanks to Black Cloud, Engine Joe and me, I'm Roy, for saving the town.

The secret celebration consists of most of the able bodied citizens of Gold Beach riding log rounds across a flat field. They have races for all ages. It takes a lot of foot work and good balance to roll the big disks across the meadow. It always happens late at night by campfire light. All roads to the area are blocked off so the secret event will never be discovered.

Now, let's see . . . it first happened in October of 1888 . . . . We normally have a pleasant fall and a mild winter, but there was a volcano somewhere across the Pacific that exploded with a bang and the sound was heard around the world. The ash cloud turned the weather around completely. When October came, the mercury dropped so fast that it bent the nails holding the thermometers. The mercury hit the bottom of the tubes so hard they broke and blew glass all over the porches. It was a comfortable 72 degrees one minute and minus 28 degrees the next. Everybody rushed home to build a fire, only to find out they were almost out of wood. They had been lulled into a false sense of security by the mild weather and had neglected to gather wood for the winter. The town was in a whole heap of trouble!

There was an old Indian camped just out of town to the south and he had a reputation for weather prediction, so the townspeople sent a committee to seek his advice. They found the shaman in a small tent not far from the beach with a thin blanket wrapped around his tall, gaunt frame.

His name was Black Cloud and he told them he could see the future and knew much of nature. Many of the councilmen scoffed at him, but others said, "What do we have to lose?"

Black Cloud built a small medicine fire and then cleared a flat place in front of it. Next, he took a little poke from around his neck, opened it and threw a collection of small bones on the ground. The old Indian studied the bones intently. He then produced a flat drum from his tent and started to tap it rhythmically with a little rattle. A low wailing chant began deep in his throat and then he seemed to go into a trance.

After a few minutes some of the men left shaking their heads in disgust.

Moments later Black Cloud looked up and spoke: "The spirits have granted three days of fair weather, then three moons of solid water – it will be the winter of a hundred seasons." As he spoke, the rays of the sun began to warm the faces of those gathered around the Indian's tent. They all looked at each other in disbelief. He then said, "Is Rogue River Roy around?" One of the men said that I had come into town a couple days ago with my mule train and he thought I was still there.

"Tell him to bring me four warm blankets," Black Cloud said. Then he continued his chant and drum tapping.

Upon their return to town, they spotted my mules behind the Port Hole Cafe and went in. I was in the back room having a piece of Apple Pie and milk. It was my favorite meal and I hated to be interrupted.

It was well known that I was a fierce man in a gunfight, but I was slow to anger. I was never one to start a fight, but then I was not one to back down either. I had a reputation for settling disputes and I was honest and treated all men as equals.

I was finishing my last bite of Apple Pie and was in an excellent mood. Pushing my chair back and rocking on its hind legs, I hooked my thumbs in my suspenders and said, "I never met an Apple Pie I didn't like." Then I looked over the group of men standing with their hats' in their hands, picked out one, and said, "What's on your mind, Mike?"

They told me what Black Cloud had said and

waited for my reply. After contemplating the situation for a few minutes, I told them, "Go find Engine Joe and tell him to meet me at the old Indian's camp. As far as the Indian is concerned, you better listen up. He's a crafty old codger and not to be scoffed at." Engine Joe was not a man to trifle with, either.

Mike Cannon, the Mayor, said "Get any provisions you need from Dan's hardware Store. The town will stand good for it."

*   *   *

Engine Joe and I met with Black Cloud and hatched a plan that would supply all the firewood the town needed for the coming winter. Then we went to Dan's Hardware Store and Dan gave us two cases of hurricane lanterns, a can of lamp oil, two barrels of hard cider, ten decks of playing cards, forty-nine "dollar" pocket watches, a chit good for four pairs of caulk boots, four Hudson Bay blankets, two hundred feet of half-inch rope, a box of spikes and a small hammer. We loaded the mules and headed up the Rogue River canyon a little after noon.

It just so happened that there were two logging camps about sixteen miles upstream. The men in these camps were in direct competition with each other and always feuding about something. Each camp had about twenty loggers, a cook and two helpers. Joe went to one camp and I showed up at the other about sundown.

I accepted the hospitality of the camp and

joined them for supper. Now, a logging camp at meal-time is a real treat. The food is outstanding and watching big burly men with sawdust-covered clothes roar through a meal like a swarm of locusts is a sight to behold. I sat transfixed, my plate untouched. The first logger who looked up asked if I was going to eat my dinner, but before I could answer he grabbed my food and it was gone in a flash. It turned out O.K. though because the cook brought out ten Apple Pies for dessert. I slid half a pie onto my plate and ate it all. To return the favor, I brought in a barrel of cider and passed out the cards, and they all sat down to play and talk.

It didn't take long for me to steer the conversation around to who was the best faller and bucker of the bunch. One outfit was called "The Wild Bunch," after the owner, I. M. Wilds. The other outfit was called "Empty Pockets," for their owner M. T. Pocket. Soon an argument started as to who was the fastest man with a misery whip.

At just the right moment, I suggested a contest, right there and then. There was an old snag on a hill above the river that was so tall the top was always in the clouds. It was over three hundred feet to the first branch and hardly any taper to the trunk at all. It was an excellent tree for a contest. In addition to the bucking, I would drive a stake into the ground and if they could hit it when they felled the tree, I promised I'd give a pocket watch to the faller. They all agreed to have the "Saw-Off" first thing in the morning. I told him this was the Wild Bunch, they'd have it tonight – there's no sissies over there in that other camp. Why, I even offered a case of lanterns in case any of them was afraid of the dark. Then I smiled so these rough and tumble loggers wouldn't take offense.

I drove the stake in the ground so the tree would fall parallel to the river. Now, this was no ordinary tree. No sir. This tree was over sixteen feet through at the butt and it would be quite a feat to fall it in the dark, even with lanterns burning brightly turning night into day.

It was such a big job that they formed a relay to make the undercut and start the backcut. It took over two hours and a huge pile of chips before the wedges were hammered in and the giant crashed to the ground. It came down with a thundering roar. The ground shook and the dust took a half hour to settle.

The men were looking for the stake when they heard a big commotion coming through the woods. It was the Wild Bunch and Engine Joe, their twenty lanterns blazing in the night, coming to see what the ruckus was about. Now, there was going to be a fight! Because every time these two outfits met there was an argument and the fists flew.

If you want to talk about real men, hard men, strong men, this is where you can find them. All these loggers were as tough as the bottoms of their hob-nailed boots. They would fight at the drop of a hat – and furnish the hat.

As expected, two of these hotheads started

swinging at each other, but before it could spread, their feet left the ground!

Engine Joe had them both by the scruff of the neck. He spoke quietly, but firmly: "Now, there is a better way to settle this, don't you agree." They both hung there, fists still clenched, nodding their heads in agreement.

A contest was soon devised. With my help, they would mark off the lower end of the giant tree into sixteen-inch lengths. Then they paired-up and raced to see who could saw the fastest. They sawed late into the night, while the cooks and volunteers kept the coffee and sandwiches coming. It must've been three in the morning when it came down to the last two teams.

The giant old snag was some what dry and dulled those bucking saws pretty fast. Nevertheless, they had just about cut that entire tree into large rounds, with only two to go.

All the loggers were gathered around the Larson brothers from the Wild Bunch and Oly Olson and Pete Peterson from the Empty Pockets outfit. Their saws were sharpened and glistened in the lamplight. The tension mounted and last minute bets were made. Both teams were stripped to the waist. Silence fell over the group, as I raised my hand. The muscular forearms of the big men bulged in anticipation. All eyes focused on the raised hand.

"Go!" . . . I shouted, as my hand fell in a chopping motion.

Both teams got off to a smooth start – no jabbing in with these experienced woodsmen. All you could hear was the swish of the saw as it bit into the wood. The sweat streamed down their muscular, saw-dust-covered arms, as they pulled the twenty-foot saw through the giant tree in a rhythm known only to loggers.

The saws kept a swishing-hum going for over forty minutes and they were still neck-n-neck. Then the Larson brothers started to fade. Soon they were over two inches behind and not likely to catch up to two tough old partners like Oly and Pete.

I thought back to when I first used to cross-buck with my Dad on the old family homestead in Missouri. *Let the saw do the work*, I could still hear my Pa say. You only pull on a crosscut, never push. That's what they mean by "pulling your weight." Well, Big Lars felt a little extra pull coming from Little Lars and soon they were picking up the pace. The younger brother had reached deep inside himself and found some inner-strength he had never tapped be-fore. Not to be outdone, his big brother's pride for little Lars swelled his heart to perform beyond his capabilities. A murmur rippled across the gathering as they realized what was happening.

The confident look on the faces of the Empty Pockets boys faded, as they grimly continued with-out letting up. With only a few inches to go, the broth-ers were coming on fast. It was going to be close. Both camps were cheering. The saws were a blur. Then there was a simultaneous crack . . . and both rounds fell off at the same instant.

A moment of silence . . . then an explosion of sound, as each camp cheered its victors. Each camp thought it had won. There was going to be trouble! Angry words were exchanged!

Bang! . . . A blinding flash! I stood with my Army Colt smoking in my hand. Now I had their attention. "It was a tie," I said. "I've never seen a better fought contest, but darn, it was a tie." There was some mumbling, but when I added, "Every man in both camps will get a brand-new pocket watch and each of the four winners will get a new pair of caulk boots," they all cheered.

Black Cloud stepped out of the shadows, startling some of the men. He calmly began to pass out the watches – cooks and volunteers included.

"Now, if you gentlemen would be so kind as to assist me in rolling these rounds down to the river I would really appreciate it," I said.

It so happened that the outhouse was located about a hundred yards down hill from the huge tree. It was right between the river and the rounds. Somebody shouted, "A dollar to the man that hits the moon cottage," and the contest was on! Those rounds came thundering down the hill like hornets headed home to the nest. They careened and bounced along toward the rickety old building. Some even bounced right over it, but not one scored a direct hit. There was only one round left. Oly lined it up very carefully and gave a steady push with a real good follow-through.

Everyone gasped as the outhouse door unexpectedly opened and one of the cooks, Harley Hansen, came staggering out. He started to say something, but then he caught sight of the huge round coming at him out of the rising sun. Before the spring-loaded door could bang shut, Harley zipped down that hill just ahead of the rolling round and dove into the river, barely escaping with his life.

The story was told for many years about how the fastest man in all the logging camps was Harley Hansen, the cook for the Wild Bunch.

The men all had a great Saturday night without any fights and headed for the bunkhouses to sleep Sunday away.

*   *   *

Meanwhile down on the river bank Joe and I were rounding up the rounds. We drove a spike into each one and roped them all together. Then we started our *herd* of logs down the Rogue River Canyon. It was the most fun we'd had in a long time.

Jumping from round to round, shooting the rapids, we were almost hysterical from laughter by the time we got to Gold Beach. We had ourselves back in control by the time we landed on the sandbar and corralled all those big, wood discs so we could roll them into town.

It didn't take long for a big crowd to form. In those days people pitched in and helped without being asked. It took about seven men to stand one of the big discs on end, but only two to roll one. While everyone was rolling them down Main Street, a few daring young men rode the roll to the top and balanced there, keeping the log rolling like a dry land log-rolling contest. They quickly became quite adept and rolled the logs right into the yards of the happy families of Gold Beach, where they could be split up for firewood.

And that solved the Great Winter of 1888 firewood shortage and saved all the people of our fair city. Until this day, people still like of it. Now, don't you tell anyone if you see'em.

THE END

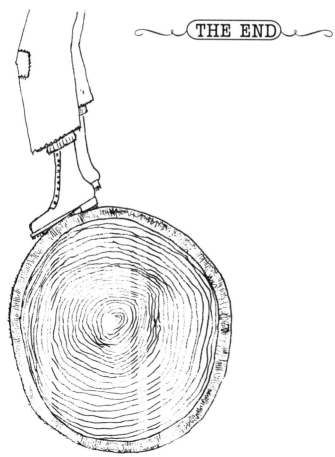

TALE SEVENTEEN
THE SNORING BABY

The rafters shook and the shakes slid off the roof, while the new Baby Boy slept peacefully through the night. Canning jars shattered in the root cellar ten feet below. The putty holding in the windows cracked and turned to dust while the onslaught continued. Lamps were being lit all over the valley, as the pioneering families woke to a most frightening noise.

Within the hour, the Jackson County Sheriff was pounding on the rough-hewn door of the little cabin. "Mr. Blaring, Mr. Blaring; is everything O.K. in there?" The latch lifted and Sheriff Will Ketchem stepped into the one-room, lantern-lit cabin.

In the yellow light, he saw before him a sleepy-eyed man and a woman with dark circles under her eyes. She was leaning against the support post and she looked totally exhausted. They both had pillows strapped around their heads covering their ears.

Near the stove was a homemade crib with a bundle of blankets in it. The sheriff stepped over to the crib and gently lifted the pale blue blanket, expecting to see a pretty little baby. But instead, an ear-shattering blast knocked his hat off and drove him back a step. Then all the windows blew out at the same time, as the hammer on his holstered Navy Colt fell on a percussion cap and fired a ball into his boot.

"@#$$%&*," yelled the sheriff. Then he hopped out of the cabin and sat down on the steps. He called for a lantern to examine his foot and Mr. Blaring brought him one, along with an apology.

As he eased his boot off, he was surprised to see that the ball had just grazed his foot. It would be black and blue for awhile, but that was better than a hole in your foot. The sheriff limped out to his skittish horse and rode back to town. *These settlers' troubles are beginning,* he mused. *If a baby can snore that loud, heaven help us when he gets old and fat and sleeps on his back.*

Sheriff Ketchem was right. The chickens quit laying eggs and the rooster couldn't stand the competition at dawn, so he struck out for new scratchings. There is nothing sadder than a rejected, whimpering rooster heading off into the sunrise. The milk cow dried up and the Blarings' faithful dog Barney slunk over the mountains to the west with his tail between his legs. Maybe he was hoping to find some peace and quite among the crashing waves of the South Coast.

All the game animals left the upper Rogue Valley. Finally, the Blarings' sleepless neighbors could take the deafening noise no longer. Their cattle had stampeded and the spring crop of corn was blown flat during the night. The new crop refused to come out of the ground – this was surely a disaster in the making.

As most of the people in the county were presenting a petition to the sheriff, a delegation arrived from the village of Medford, with yet another petition. The Blarings were fine people, but the pressure brought to bear by everyone within twenty-six miles was overwhelming. They would have to leave.

Sheriff Ketchem rode out to the Blarings' farm and informed them of their eviction. They were very upset, but knew only too well the problem their little baby was causing. As an inducement to leave the area, the sheriff handed Ulysses R. Blaring, Sr. a leather pouch with gold coins in it amounting to twice the value of their farm. In addition, a wagon would be delivered the next day and a group of neighbors would help them load it with their belongings.

Little U. R. Blaring, Jr. took that moment to fall asleep and he let out a snore that knocked the sheriff's hat off and caused the hammer on his revolver to fall on an empty chamber. Ketchem was not a slow learner. His horse broke away from the hitching post and high-tailed it for town. The only livestock Blaring had left was a matched pair of white horses, both of them stone deaf. Blaring offered one of the horses, Snowball, to the sheriff, so he could ride back to town on the condition that the sheriff would return the horse the next morning with the wagon.

As the departing Blarings drove through town on their way to Grants Pass, little U. R. fell asleep from the rocking of their new YELLOW WAGON. The shock wave from his first snore knocked over the blacksmith's anvil, as he was swinging a large hammer, causing him to miss and hit his leg instead.

The furious man limped outside, yelling "!@#$%&, and *&^%$#@," but when he saw the pretty, little baby, it melted his hard blacksmith's heart. He was starting to koochy-coo the tiny infant, when another blast knocked him down and blew the fire in his forge all over the shop, starting it ablaze. The good people of the Town of Rogue River responded to the alarm and put the fire out rapidly with a bucket brigade.

The YELLOW WAGON left town quickly.

On the way to Grants Pass, they crossed the Burly North railroad tracks as a steam-locomotive billowing black smoke and shaking the ground rolled up to the crossing. The Engineer blew his ear-shattering whistle. The intense vibrations and white steam startled the horses of the Blarings' nearby wagon and caused the horses to run. The train crew all laughed at their dangerous joke. Then little U. R. Blaring let loose a blast of his own and the huge locomotive swayed on the tracks like a rocking, iron horse! Fortunately, all of the crew was able to bail out on the high side. As the second snore blasted forth, the huge machine was blown on its side, to the amazement of the dumbfounded crew.

The little YELLOW WAGON left the scene quickly.

Now, the telegraph was a wonderful invention, but for some, it was a messenger of distress. The Engineer had wired ahead with warnings about the little YELLOW WAGON and its disruptive occupant, so the Town of Grants Pass had been forewarned of the eminent danger they faced. The railroad said they would rip up their tracks and leave the area if the little YELLOW WAGON was permitted to stay in town. The Burly North said they were businessmen and couldn't afford to go around putting locomotives back on the tracks every day. They had nothing personal against the little baby, but he would have to move on.

Now, Grants Pass had a big sign at the edge of town that said "Welcome to Grants Pass it's the Friendly Climate!" The "Committee to Preserve Sanity" quickly removed the words "Welcome" and "Friendly" from the sign before the little YELLOW WAGON arrived in town.

A delegation of men – they were more like vigilantes – greeted (blocked the road) the wagon at the city limits. They started out by threatening the little family, but then Jr. Blaring cut loose with a noise so horrible it would make the hair on a razorback hog stand on end. Those who were left standing quickly started to negotiate. The vigila . . . err . . . ah . . . Committee offered a sum of one hundred dollars, gold, if they would bypass the town and keep on going.

The couple accepted the generous offer on the condition that the townspeople provide milk for their baby. The quite relieved council quickly agreed and sent for a milk cow to tag along behind their rig. It was an all-white cow and totally deaf, but a good milker. It was a perfect match for the Blarings. A volunteer who was also deaf offered to guide the YELLOW WAGON around the town.

* * *

Meanwhile, the Waymen brothers, Rob and Hiram, were watching the encounter from the back of the crowd. A more evil duo had never existed. The shadowy pair watched the gold change hands – their eyes never left the bulging purse. They saw Ulysses stash the gold in a strongbox under the seat, wave to the crowd and start off on the bypass around the town. Without a word spoken, the brothers mounted their horses and headed for town. If the YELLOW WAGON was going around the town, they would get ahead of them and cut 'em off at Balancing Rock pass.

They had the ambush ready long before the wagon arrived. Their plan was to shoot one horse and the driver; that way they couldn't get away. Then shoot the woman and other horse, leaving no witnesses. The brothers lay on the ground behind their rifles shaking with anticipation, eager for the gold to arrive. What a dastardly pair of cold - blooded killers. Soon they heard the clatter of hooves and the jingle of the harness, as the two faithful animals came closer to their doom.

The YELLOW WAGON came round the bend and as the brothers took careful aim, the helpless targets kept coming closer. Then they took the slack out of the triggers, held their breath, and BLAM! The blast from the *baby* knocked their hats off their heads and their aim off the target. Both rifles discharged together, missing completely. They hadn't counted on little Jr. Blaring being asleep.

The bandits were starting to reload, when they heard a rumble behind them. Balancing Rock had become unbalanced from the baby's blast and it was rolling and bouncing right in their direction! Stunned at the sight of a fifty-ton boulder bounding towards them, they froze in their tracks. There was nowhere to go! But before the giant rock could smash them, they jumped off the cliff! "Ahhhhhhh and Ahhhhhhh!" they screamed as they fell.

They landed in a big cedar tree growing out of a crack in the rock wall and were starting to smile at their good fortune, when the huge boulder came crashing down right on top of them. They were never seen in that part of the country again, thus ending the dastardly careers of Rob and Hi Waymen.

The little YELLOW WAGON quickly left the area.

Every town they came to had already heard about the YELLOW WAGON and the word put out by the Burly North Railroad. Suddenly it dawned on them that in the olden days, *yellow* was the color used to warn people of the Black Plague sickness and that's why the kind people had painted their wagon yellow.

*   *   *

They camped that night with little hope of ever finding a place they could settle down. When they awoke in the morning, their campfire was already burning brightly. An old Indian was cooking bacon and eggs and golden brown biscuits. Mrs. Blaring didn't know quite what to do. She had heard tales of savage Indians murdering pioneers and stealing their horses. She said tentatively, "How?"

"Oh, I just mixed up a little sourdough I carry with me and added some milk from your white cow and voila, here it is. These are the best biscuits ever. I learned the recipe from an old muleskinner named Rogue River Roy, down on the river of the same name. That's where I'm headed."

"Why you speak perfect English! I thought you were a savage."

"Sorry to disappoint you, Madam, but I haven't had any savage thoughts since my tribe sent me away almost thirty years ago," said the old Indian. "Excuse my manners. My name is "Black Cloud," and I'm from a tribe far to the east. I am a Medicine Man and can tell the future for some and cast spells for others."

"I must apologize, too, Mr. Black Cloud. Welcome to our campsite. I'm Mrs. Blaring and this is my husband, Ulysses." She nodded to the man beside her, who was lowering his Winchester.

Over breakfast, the campers exchanged stories. Black Cloud told them how he was schooled by French Missionaries and could speak both French and English.

The Blarings told him of their troubles. They said they were at their wit's end trying to figure out what to do, because everyone kept telling them to move on.

Black Cloud said he had heard the singing wires tell of their plight and offered his help. Of course, they accepted. The old Indian gathered a few special twigs and bark and then made a small fire near a hard, flat place. Then he retrieved a small, flat drum from his deerskin pack. Next, he took a small leather pouch from around his neck, which was filled with little bones and he cast them upon the dry earth. He added some green cascara leaves and fanned the flames with the drum until a cloud of smoke arose from the fire.

From low in his throat came forth a melodious chant that filled the morning air as he tapped on the ancient drum. The Blarings watched the ceremony, spellbound by Black Cloud's performance.

After a few minutes, he stopped and smiled at the young couple. "You will travel west to the big lake and there you will find a point of land that extends out into the blue water. Upon this land you will find a place to dwell and there will be peace. I'm going in the same direction and will guide you, if you don't mind the company of a savage!"

Mrs. Blaring blushed. "Not at all – we would greatly appreciate your help."

So, the small company headed off through the mountains towards the grand Pacific Ocean. About three weeks later, they arrived at fair-sized prominence called "Mute Point." To their joy and amazement, there was Barney – their dog, who had run away earlier in this tale – doing what a dog loves most: chasing seagulls on the beach. The first morning, Black Cloud stole the little dog's heart when he gave him some biscuits dipped in bacon grease. They were inseparable from that point on.

The Blarings parted company with Black Cloud after thanking him for all his help. They gave him a container of milk to make more biscuits and told him to stop in whenever he traveled their way, as he would always be welcome. The old Indian and the little dog disappeared into the forest and headed for Port Orford to the south, as the Blarings waved goodbye.

*   *   *

The newly arrived settlers built a cabin on a high cliff with a glorious view of the ocean. The baby's room was on the ocean side of the cabin in a kinda' tower, so the crashing waves would help muffle the sound of his snoring. It worked perfectly. In fact, during the foggy days not a single ship went aground on the treacherous shore. The year before the Blarings arrived, six vessels had been wrecked on the rocks, and the year before that, seven ships had been sunk within sight of the little cabin. During the following years, not one ship had the misfortune to end up on the dangerous shores. By the time little U. R. Blaring was ten years old, the government and the shipping companies were paying the young man a handsome fee to sleep when it was foggy. The family used the money to buy most of Mute Point. They eventually had one of the largest sheep ranches in the State of Oregon.

Mute Point was so misnamed that the locals renamed it "Cape Blanco Hombre Ronquido." Translated from Spanish this means: "White man snoring." It was later shortened to "Cape Blanco."

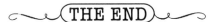

THE END

As told to Rogue River Roy
by his good friend Black Cloud.

This brings to an end a few of the stories from the journal of Rogue River Roy. The following story was written by Dr. Lewis Cannon vainly trying to copy the truthfulness, honesty and integrity of Rogue River Roy.

TALE EIGHTEEN
"DOUBLE TROUBLE" A FISH STORY

I've heard a lot of fish stories in my time, living here on the Rogue River as I do, but this one is the absolute truth. I know for sure, because it happened to me. This tale is so strange I don't have to lie or even stretch the truth. Now, the real beginning was when I was about ten years old and was watching a lightning storm with my Pa and older brother. It was a hellacious storm and went on most of the night. It had snowed the day before and it made the lightning just brilliant. Some of the lightning bolts came from the sky down; some came from the ground up; and some went from cloud to cloud.

When we saw one bolt that went up, down and back and forth, my Pa said, "That's how you can tell if it coming right at you or going the other way." My brother and I both ducked. Pa chuckled. "You got to be quicker than that, boys. Lucky it was going the other way."

Lucky for me I always listened to my Pa, because about two and a half years later I was watching a meteor shower in August. It looked like it was raining shooting stars. They all had sparkling tails behind them. Except one that kinda wandered a little and kept getting bigger and BIGGER! All of a sudden, I remembered what my Pa had said, and I realized it was coming right at me!

At the last second, I stepped aside and it hit right where I had been standing. Then it bounced into a mud puddle and sizzled. I waited till the steam quit coming off it and then I bent over and picked it up. The walnut-sized star was still warm and very heavy.

The next day, I took my treasure to the town blacksmith and showed it to him. "Yep!" he said. "That's a meteorite. It has a lot of nickel in it and that's why it's so heavy." He wanted to pound it into a little knife for me and said he would only charge me a dollar. I was broke, being a kid and all, so I said, "I'll just hold on to it for now." I put it in a little leather poke and carried it around my neck. Well, it was lucky I did, as you will soon find out.

On my thirteenth birthday, I got my first store-bought fishing pole and it was a Jim-Dandy. It took me about six minutes to get ready and I was heading for my favorite gravel bar on the whole Rogue River to try out my new pole. The reason it took me so long was I had to thank my folks and have a piece of cake. STRAWBERRY SHORTCAKE, my favorite! – after Apple Pie.

I'll bet I wasn't fishing more than five minutes when BANG! I had my first strike. Now, I never had a fish hit that hard, just wham! He pulled all the line off my reel before I could even blink and then kept right on going.

I stood there with a dumb expression on my face and then I looked around to see if anyone had seen my stupidity. A kingfisher sat on a nearby willow. He stared right at me and then flew away in disgust, emitting a call that sounded like, "DUMMY, DUMMY, DUMMY."

I raced back home and filled my reel with forty-pound test line, the heaviest I had ever used on a Chinook salmon. I'll bet it wasn't six minutes later I was back on the bar and ready to try again. I cast out to the place upstream that I had last seen that ornery monster – without any results. Then I thought I'd try the hole where I had hooked him the first time. My lure no sooner hit the water than BANG! He was hooked again. "Yahoo!" I shouted. "I'M READY FOR YOU THIS TIME."

He took off upstream with a rooster tail of water coming off the line. I thumbed the spool with the leather brake pad. As the line began to disappear, I felt my heart beating in my throat. I was excited and fearful of losing this giant fish. I was just about out of line when everything stopped. Then, before I realized it, he was heading back downstream. I recovered some line as he passed me, still in deep water and then he slowed as I was running out of line. This went on for about two hours: upstream, downstream and then suddenly the line snapped. Zing! It went sailing past my head. When I reeled in, it wasn't the line, but the hook. It had just broken in two. *Well, I'll be,* I said to myself. It was quite puzzling.

I took the hook to Pa and he said, "Get a bigger hook." So I went to the Outdoor Store and bought a bigger hook. Everyone in the store kinda snickered when they saw the size hook I wanted, but I said, "Just you wait!"

I'll bet it wasn't ten minutes later, I was back after an even larger hook. This time they chuckled out loud and I left a little red-faced. The next time I entered the store, the store clerk put a boat anchor on the counter and all the customers "hooted" me out the door. I was so mad I was fit-to-be-tied. I yelled back over my shoulder, "You just wait!" (Or something equally clever). I guess I didn't know how to take a joke yet, after all I was only a kid.

Well, to make a short story long, I wore out about a half-dozen hooks trying to catch that huge fish, but he never broke the water, not even once.

Then it came to me as I was fondling the little pouch around my neck. I took the broken hooks to the blacksmith and told him about my problem with the big fish. He said, "Yep, metal fatigue. You need a tougher hook, not a bigger one." I showed him my meteorite and he agreed to make me a hook from it. It would be the strongest, toughest, sharpest hook in the whole of these United States and it wouldn't cost me a dime, only half the fish, IF I landed it. It was a DEAL and he started to work on the meteorite hook.

He heated, pounded and hammered that little star till the sparks were flying and the forge was roaring white hot. It took him about a half hour to form the hook on the anvil and then he went over to the grinding wheel to sharpen the point. I helped by turning the crank and adjusting the water drip just right. Smitty told me to watch the sparks because they tell you what kinda metal you're grinding. Sure enough, the little sparks were jumping off and forking and forking again like little shooting stars. It was like the Fourth of July!

When he got it sharp enough to make a scratch on his thumbnail, he reheated the point to a cherry red, waited a second and plunged it into some oil. He held up the hook, looked it over real good and said, "Perfect!" I thanked him for the hook and headed back to the gravel bar.

Then I remembered I had my chores to do and I was torn between fishing and working. Doing what you're supposed to do and not what you want to do is part of growing up, so I went home.

At the crack of dawn, it was back to the bar. I cast right into that same hole. WHAM! Darned if I didn't hook that slab on the first cast, you'd think he was homesteading in there. I yelled, "Fish on," because there were several *good-old-boys* nearby. They all pulled their gear and stepped back to watch the show. Evidently word had spread about the monster fish and the kid fisherman, because quite a crowd had gathered to watch.

It was as if that fish was waiting for me. No! Not waiting! Playing with me! He was beginning to get my goat! He was upstream and downstream, back and forth, time and time again, but at least the hook held. I'd never seen the like before.

Now, all you old fishermen know that a fish can't breathe when he's swimming fast. He closes his gills and makes his run. Then he stops to rest and catch his breath. That's when you take in a little line and wait for the next run. Every run the fish makes is a little less than the one before. Soon he's tuckered out and you just reel him in. Now, that's how you catch a big fish on a little line.

Well, evidently this fish was from a different school than the rest of them, as he kept it up without slacking off one bit. He kept it up for fourteen hours straight. I was getting hungry; my arms were like lead pipes; and my back felt like I was being branded. An old fisherman stood nearby and gave me a lot of advice. He even offered to take over so I could rest and eat. I thanked him and said, "I'll just tough it out."

Then I got a break. The sun was low on the horizon and I was losing the light, when that feisty fish ran smack dab into a rock. He was a little upstream when it happened and I was reeling in like mad. Another fisherman ran out and tried to net him for me.

"He's too big for the net," he said. Then he reached down and grabbed the fish and started to drag him up onto the gravel bar. "You're not going to believe this! You're just not going to believe this!"

Well, he was right. It was the darndest thing I had ever seen. I just couldn't believe it. There were two giant salmon joined at the belly! One was pointed upstream and one was pointed downstream – like a Siamese fighting fish.

So, that's why the fish never stopped to rest. He rolled over when he got tired and the other one went full speed in the other direction. *Well, I'll be jiggered,* I thought.

What a great day it was. I had finally caught that fish, the biggest one anyone had ever seen and I was only a kid. One of the tourists had a camera and offered to take my picture with the fish. It took four of us to hold it up and one guy said he bet it would go three hundred pounds if it went an ounce.

I was standing there talking to the crowd and trying to figure out how to weigh this critter or critters, when the blacksmith showed up. Before anyone could say anything, he whipped out his knife and cut the fish apart. Everyone yelled at the same time, "NO!" but it was too late. The deed was done and my prize "double trouble" fish was no more. Well, a promise is a promise. I told him to enjoy his fish, as I fought back the tears. I thought this was the worst thing that had ever happened to me. Boy was I wrong!

The worst time was later, when the game warden showed up and told me the fish wasn't hooked legal, as it was the other half that took the lure and he confiscated the fish. (That meant he would have fish for dinner.) Fortunately, he didn't arrest me because I was "just a kid."

Well, what else could possibly go wrong? I found out when someone handed me my new fishing pole and it had been stepped on and the tip was broken!

Now, the good news is that the picture of me and the fish turned out great, although it was heavy – the negative alone weighed eleven pounds.

Oh yes, the blacksmith gave me back my "star" hook, but I never use it. I just keep it around to remind me of a day long ago, fishing on the Rogue.

THE END

PUBLISHERS DISCLAIMER

The people at Moon House Publishing are
very reluctant to put into print this outrageous
book as it is a total pack of lies. None of the
characters here within have any basis in truth
and even the author is fictional. As we found out
when we tried to collect the money he owes us.
If by chance you are unfortunate enough to meet
This scoundrel please notify
MOON HOUSE PUBLISHING COMPANY.